FIVE CHANCES

FIVE CHANCES

Mike Pringle

Published in Great Britain by Green Rook 2014

www.greenrook.co.uk

Text and cover illustration © 2014 Mike Pringle

ISBN 978-0-9930524-0-8

To Claire, Charlie, Jasper and Andrew,
for inspiration, support and sound advice.

This story was inspired by a World War One poem
called 'The Chances' by Wilfred Owen (see page 243),
and is dedicated to his memory and to the other ten
million people who lost their lives during that war.

In the Great War of 1914-18, millions of men were sent to fight in the trenches of the Western Front. Many of them were under age.

They reckoned they had five chances: death, injury, capture, madness... or survival.

1. WAR

It were a bad leg day, but I didn't care. The hooter at the railway works blasted out, ten times. It were the signal I'd been waiting for. England were going to war with Germany. The Hun. And I'd get my own bed for the first time ever. Each hoot made me want to cheer out loud, but Birdy was already waiting in the backsy, the alley behind our row of houses. I sneaked out of our yard gate and he shoved a big sack at me that smelled of dead things, and told me to keep my mouth shut an follow him.

With the steam hooter still making my ears ring, I hugged along them stone walls, trying to keep up. I were dead nervy someone was going to pop out of their yard gate and catch us. And I were right to worry about that an all. The hooter had shaked up the whole works village. Most evenings it was quiet as you like, with the men back in their homes, changing out of their overalls. Tea time. Instead, folk was coming out into the backsy to talk to their neighbours about what it all meaned. The hooter going off, and the war an that.

'Can't be doin' with this,' says Birdy, clutching an even bigger sack than the one he give me. 'Just what we bleedin' needs. Come on Noggin, this way.'

He switched down the alley that leads to Bristol Street, and I limped after him, wishing the bag weren't so heavy. As we got near the end, I comed face to face with Emma Deacon with her mum an dad. Emma smiled at me. My heart stopped an I just stared like an idiot. Mr Deacon asked where we was going in such a hurry. Birdy didn't say nothing and I just mumbled something an pushed past them an out on to the street.

'We has to cut across the works to Rodbourne Cheney,' Birdy says. 'Through the tunnel. Only way to avoid all these people. Can't let them see this, can I.'

He nodded at the shotgun hanging off his shoulder. Birdy weren't daft, of course, and had it wrapped up in hessian. But I reckon anyone could figure out what it was straight off, the shape were that obvious. He didn't wait to see if I had anything to say about it. Just headed into the tunnel what led under the tracks to the railway works.

I didn't want to go to the works, nor anywhere

near 'em. Didn't even want to step through that archway into the tunnel. But I did, and it were dark in there, with the summer evening light left outside. Birdy was already a good few yards off, and I knew I were going to struggle to keep pace with him. I had good days and bad days with my leg, and today was a bad leg day, for sure. That hot feeling were working its way up from my foot before I even sneaked out the house. I knowed the stiffness would be there soon.

'Birdy,' I says, not wanting to speak too loud like.

But he didn't hear. A bang off to the side made me near jump out of my skin. That made Birdy look my way. It were just one of the counter girls, slamming the wooden shutter on her little arched window. Her job were done now 'til tomorrow morning.

'What you waiting for?' says Birdy, and I could tell he were irritated.

A whole load of things popped into my head what I wanted to say. For one thing, we shouldn't have been going into the works at all. It were against the rules, and Birdy knowed that. Them Company watchmen was right nasty pieces of work. They'd haul you up for near anything, just out of spite. And for another thing, Mam and Grandma, and Uncle Phil an Auntie Jean, would be at home all chattering about how come I'd sneaked out just when war was announced, and before teatime an all. Dad would be set to give me a hiding. Especially if he thought I was up to no good. Which I was.

But it weren't just them things. Deep down inside, I had a remembering of something fearful in them works. I don't know if it were a remembering of something real, or just of things what Mam and Dad or Jim had told me here and there. Whatever it was, I couldn't help them horrid feelings growing inside me whenever I thought about the works. A gurgling in my belly. Dark shadows flitting about in my head.

In the end, I used a different excuse, which was true.

'It's my leg,' I says, clutching at my bad 'un. 'It ain't working right.'

Birdy took a pace back towards me. Sticks his pointy chin out.

'Well, stamp it then,' he says, in a whisper that weren't far off being a growl. 'I ain't got time for this.'

Turning, he starts off down the tunnel, his skinny body just a dark shape against the light from the other end. It made his ears look like they was sticking out even more an normal. I dumped the sack of dead rabbits down so I could use both hands to lift my leg up, took in a breath, an stamped my foot down onto the flagstones. The noise echoed along the tunnel, and I quickly looked back to the ticket windows. But there weren't nobody there. I gived my foot a quick shake, and the hot feeling faded a bit. Picking up the bag again, I walked forward, swinging my legs nice and straight. Just like the Doctor says I must.

Birdy were about half way along, and didn't look back. I reckon he were thinking to go without me. If I'm truthful about it, that's probably what he thinked right from the start. And I don't blame him none. Most times, Jim, my big brother, would help him out when he had stuff that needed moving. Even though Jim said Birdy were daft for doing them things. But they'd been friends ever since Birdy came to Town looking for work, after his family's farm went bust, an Jim put up with his ways. I only said I'd go 'cause Jim were at Technical School with the other railway apprentices that evening. It were stupid of me to think I could take his place. After all, Birdy's little *sideline*, as he called it, were way too important to risk being messed up by my rotten leg. Them dead birds an rabbits an stuff was everything to him. Shot with his dad's old gun, or caught in traps, and selled to the workers. Including us. Even though trading in the works village were against Company rules. Birdy didn't care about that, mind. Said his family needed the money.

Even so, I were still an idiot to say I'd help him move 'em, 'specially since he had the gun with him an all. I couldn't even be sure the dead game was his to sell neither. Most folk reckoned Birdy didn't always go shooting on legal lands, an poaching were a proper crime. Prison. Even us Townies knowed that. To make it worse, now we had to go through the railway works. The worst place of all to be caught red handed.

Marching down the tunnel, I tried to keep my mind on better things. Like the war, and what that would mean at home. A bed of my own for one thing. My very own, at last. But I weren't able to think about that for long. Birdy cussed, and I looked up. The evening sunlight at the far end goes dark all of a sudden like. There was a small crowd of bodies coming in. I couldn't see proper, on account of Birdy being in front of me, but I weren't that bothered. If it were the watchmen coming to lock up the tunnel, all we had to do was turn around and set off back out the way we came. We'd be gone in no time, even with my leg. They might shout at us, but they wouldn't come after us since we hadn't got to the works yet. Not even the nastiest of 'em. At least that's what I reckoned.

For a moment, I thought Birdy figured the same thing. He turned back and comes towards me. Then I sees his face. His eyes was wide and staring, and his mouth were trying to make words but without speaking none. I looked beyond him, full expecting to see them old watchmen standing there, ready to lock the gates. But it weren't the watchmen at all. It were half a dozen lads. Straight off, I knowed the shape of the person in the middle. Smaller than the rest of 'em, but strutting like he were the biggest of 'em all, wiry muscles flexing on his arms. He shouted out, and I heared that sharp, crystal clear voice. It were William Adams, and I reckon he were a worse person to run into than any of them watchmen. Worse by a long shot.

2. BIRDY'S GUN

Adams was on us in no time, and his mates. Five of 'em. Birdy probably could have legged it and made it out the tunnel before they got to us. In fact, not probably. Easily. But he knowed I never had a chance. I hated my leg all the time. But there was some times when I hated it even more.

'Well,' says Adams, his laugh as sharp as his speaking voice. 'What've we got here then? Couple of trespassers, is it? Maybe we should call the watchmen. What d'you reckon lads?'

Course his mates laughed at that, but they didn't say nothing. Knowed there weren't no point in speaking when Adams was. More than their lives was worth. Birdy still had his back to 'em, and waved his hand at me.

'Just go,' he says, taking the sack off me and placing both of 'em down. 'Go on. I'll see to this. They ain't interested in you none.'

He pulled on the strap of the wrapped up gun, and turned an faced Adams and his mates. Even in the dinginess I seed Adams's green eyes sparkling. Them eyes caught mine, just for a flash. I felt like he could see right into me, see something awful about me that made him want to laugh out loud. I moved backwards, real slow like. My leg were stiffening up something bad, and my guts feeled like they was going to spill all over them tunnel flagstones. But Birdy was right. Adams's eyes switched to him. He didn't do nothing about me and nor did his mates. Like I weren't there. Didn't hardly exist at all. Instead, Adams spotted the package hanging off Birdy's shoulder, an grabbed out at it before Birdy had a chance to know what were happening.

'Here,' Birdy shouted, trying to grab it back. 'Get off that. Leave it.'

But Adams paid no heed, and grappled with Birdy for the gun. In a second, his pals were there an all, pinning Birdy's arms away from the gun, and helping their leader to take it for himself.

'Well, I'll be damned,' says Adams, tugging off the hessian wrappings. 'I could've sworn this were a poacher's gun. But look, it ain't at all. It's some bleedin' antique. You'd be better off throwing this at a rabbit than trying to shoot him with it.'

Adams's mates laughed at that, of course. But it was true the shotgun was old. It were a flintlock, and looked like it were about a hundred year old or more, rusted and caked with black oily muck. But to Birdy it was his only way of getting food for his family, an the one thing that freed him up some from his poor life.

'Just hand it back, Adams,' he says, and his voice were shaking. 'It ain't yours. Give it here.'

Adams's face switched from the gun, to Birdy, then to me again.

'You still here?' He says to me. 'Do yourself a favour cripple boy, and do like your pal here says. Go on, begger off.'

I knowed I had no choice, and turned an headed for the tunnel entrance, half expecting to get something chucked at me when I showed 'em my back. And hating what he called me.

As I hobbled off, I couldn't hear proper what was being said behind me. But I knew it weren't good. Not for Birdy anyhow. Him an Adams had never seen eye to eye. Adams worked as a labourer inside the works, hotting rivets in the Boiler Shop where Dad worked. And Dad says Adams didn't take kindly to other lads what weren't in his gang, especially them what had sidelines that he weren't gaining from. On top of that, he hated country boys more than any other.

When I were back near the ticket hatches, a loud

noise from down the tunnel made me stumble. I just about stopped myself falling over, and ducked behind the iron pillars holding up the roof there. Even though I didn't want to know what were happening, I couldn't help it, and peeked out to look back. Them figures was all just dark shapes, but it were easy still to make out Birdy an Adams. They was about the same height, and just as thin as each other. Though where Birdy was spindly and underfed, Adams were lean and muscled. Birdy was being holded by Adams's big mates, and Adams were swinging the gun up above his head. My first thinking was he were going to beat Birdy with it. But he didn't. He smashed it down on the flagstones instead. Again an again he crashed the thing down, each time bits flying off. One more time and what was left of the gun just fell apart, so there just weren't no gun to talk of no more. Adams were left holding the barrel, bent and misshaped. He juggled it in his hands for a minute, then hurled it down the tunnel, skidding along the flagstones towards my hiding place. He laughed, right in Birdy's face.

Before Birdy had a chance to react any, Adams an his mates turned on him. I pulled back behind the pillars, so I couldn't see no more. My breathing was going like a steam hammer, but the noise of it in an out of my chest couldn't hide them sounds from down the tunnel. At first it was just a dull thumping, part hidden under shouting an swear words from Adams and his mates. And from Birdy an all, to start with. Then there were a yelp, shaking off the tunnel walls like some wild animal were being killed. I feeled sick to my stomach. I had an urge to look out to see what had happened, but I didn't dare. I knowed it was Birdy. Knowed they was getting the better of him. I pulled back flat as I were able against the wall, my leg shaking under me.

'Come on, Noggin,' I says to myself, tapping my bad heel against the flagstones. 'Use your brain. That's what God give it you for. Come on. What're you going to do?'

Course, I knew the answer really. Jim. My big brother Jim was the answer. If Jim had been there with Birdy, like usual, there weren't no way Adams would've tried anything on. Jim was much bigger than me, an bigger than any of Adams' mates. He took after Dad. From good engineering stock, Mam always says. Hands like coal shovels, and strong as an ox. I weren't a bad size, for my age, but when it came to bulk an strength, I reckon I took after Mam.

But it weren't only Jim's size that kept Adams off.

Most the time Jim were a quiet one. Never had nothing to say unless it needed saying. Kept himself to himself, and never troubled no one about a thing.

But some times that would change. Only we never knowed when, or what would set it off. Just every here an there, Jim flied into a rage. Like he were a different person altogether. Not my brother no more. Shouting and screaming, and his whole face looking like it were about to burst. I only seed it happen a few times, and only once were it at me. But it were enough. That time, he flied off the handle all because I moved the candle from the windowsill in our bedroom. I can still imagine his face twisting in front of mine, his huge voice bellowing at me and spit flying all over, an his arms waving an all. Any minute I figured he were going to start battering me, and then he'd just carry on, them huge hands like hammers beating me to death. All 'cause of a candle. I never did work out why it made him so angry, but Mam said I weren't to think about it none, and be more considerate in future. And that's how it was in the house with Jim. Mam an Dad never said nothing when he lost it. Jim would storm off to our room and just sit there staring out of the window, with his eyebrows knotted together an deep, faraway eyes ignoring everything. It would go quiet for days after, with even Uncle Phil and Auntie Jean tiptoeing about in case something sets him off again. Even Grandma. Just lucky it didn't happen too often.

Of course, Adams knowed all about Jim's temper.

Everybody did. Adams might've even seen it for himself sometimes, in the works. I don't know. But Birdy didn't have Jim to keep him safe this time. All he had was me, and I were useless to him. No good at all.

I clutched my head, and grinded my teeth together, trying to think what to do. But the only two things I could come up with was both pointless. I knowed the best thing would be to go and find Jim. He'd be back home from his class at the Technical School by now. But with my leg, it would take me best part of five minutes to get back there, and a bit for Jim to get back to the tunnel. Birdy didn't have five minutes. He didn't have no time at all.

3. JIM

My other idea was worse still. If there weren't no time to fetch help, then I'd have to give it myself. Go back an do what I could for Birdy on my own. The thought drew a taste of sick into my mouth, and tears come into my eyes. I might've come from the same family as Jim an Dad, but without their strength what good was I? Too many years pulling around a bad leg when I should've been working proper like all the other boys, building muscles.

And I were scared.

I knowed Adams an his mates would laugh at me if I tried anything. They'd beat me same as they was beating Birdy, and there weren't nothing I could do to stop 'em.

But I couldn't just leave Birdy. I had to do what I could. Something.

Stamping my heel against the floor, I tried to take

in a deep breath, but my mouth were too dry. I couldn't even swallow. I pulled myself up straight as I were able, and stared at the wall opposite me. Big solid blocks holding up the railway tracks above the roof, for the locomotives and tenders and trains and everything. On the walls of the tunnel there was cables and wires and pipes running the whole length.

Wires. A thought jumped up. Some of them was for the watchmen's bells. Two, one each end of the tunnel. The watchmen rang 'em before locking up, in case there was anyone still inside, or on their way from the works an hoping to get through. One of 'em was there right in front of me. If I could get it to ring, Adams would think the watchmen was coming. Birdy would be safe, for sure. But my heart sank again. The bell push was down the works end of the tunnel. A million miles away for my leg, and past Adams an his mates.

My head dropped, and I leaned back against the wall, staring at Birdy's gun barrel lying there, bent and beaten.

Then, real slow like, an idea creeped into my head. The barrel. It were metal. What if I could touch it across the contacts on the bell, the two brass screws holding the wires. Would the bell ring? I couldn't be sure where the electricity was coming from. It may be that nothing would happen at all. Worse than that,

I'd probably get an electric shock.

'Got to try anyway, Noggin,' I says to myself, gritting my teeth. 'For Birdy.'

I pulled out of my hiding place and strided towards the barrel. Adams shouted again, cursing Birdy for being stupid and a bumpkin an all, between the beatings and kickings they was giving him. Birdy were on the floor and weren't making no noises at all. I snatched up the barrel, taking care that I didn't stumble with my stiff leg, and carried straight on to the other side of the tunnel. All I could hear was the sound of Adams's mates laughing. I ignored it, and held the barrel behind me, ready to swing it up to the bell. But before I could do it, I heared a voice shouting behind me.

Jim near knocked me down as he went past. He ran into the tunnel, screaming at the top of his breath and going so fast he were almost at Adams before I even had time to know it were him for sure.

I dropped the barrel and tried to run after him into the tunnel, seeing him crash into Adams, fists flying and everyone shouting. The noise filled the tunnel, and made me go as fast as I'd ever gone. Fast as my leg would let me. I could feel my eyes wide and mouth open, and my heart pounding. Different feelings. I were excited 'cause Jim had come and was going to take care of everything. I was happy 'cause I weren't going to get beated up by Adams an his mates. But I were feeling let down an all, almost sad. I were so close to doing something. Something clever. At least I hoped I was. Now I'd never know.

The crowd broke up straight off. Adams's mates ran away soon as they seed their leader being beaten. Adams squirmed and twisted from Jim's blows but didn't have nothing to give in return. With his arms up to look after his face, he pulled away and ran off after his mates, out the other end of the tunnel. Jim chased them for a bit, then turned and comed back towards Birdy. A heap on the floor. I got there first and leaned down. There was blood on his face.

'Birdy, Birdy. You alright, Birdy?' I says, but I didn't get no answer.

As Jim got to us, Birdy sort of grunted and moved some. He pulled himself to his knees, real slow like. I tried to take his arm to help pull him up, but he shrugged and pulled his arm away from me, choosing to get up on his own.

Jim stood there an waited for his friend to stand up straight. They looked at each other, Jim giving a little rise of his eyebrows, like he was asking if Birdy were okay. Even though he knowed he weren't. Birdy gave back a tiny nod and headed off down the tunnel the way we first come. I seed the blood was around his eye and dripping from his nose. He didn't even look at the pieces of gun scattered about, and left the sacks of game behind.

*

I had my own bed for about five minutes I reckon. We was all sitting around waiting for Mam to come out from the scullery. I heared her coughing as she shoved the last of the day's dusty washing into the copper and stoked the fire under it. She'd sent Jim to find me. He dragged me back home, plain angry with me for going off with Birdy. And angrier still that I didn't do nothing to help Birdy against Adams. Even though I tried to explain what I were going to do, he wouldn't talk to me about it. But he didn't say nothing to Mam an Dad about what had happened neither, so at least I didn't get a hiding.

'War means changes,' Mam says, coming out an drying her hands on her pinny. 'And them changes is going to happen here an all.'

She waved a hand at us all. Dad was in his normal chair. He were watching Mam, though he couldn't hear a word she was saying. Working in the din of the Boiler Shop made most of them men deaf as doornails, and Dad had worked there almost all his life. Me an Jim was standing next to him, and Grandma was on the other chair with her arm around Auntie Jean, who was crying.

'Your Uncle Phil's gone away,' Mam carries on. 'To

do his duty. He be on the way by now, on the Midland and South West. And we should all remember him in our prayers.'

That made Auntie Jean cry even more.

I were trying real hard not to show how it was making me feel. Didn't want Mam see a smile on my face, while I were waiting for her to say what was coming next. Right from the first talkings of war, we knowed that Uncle Phil would be called up if it happened. He were a volunteer in the Yeomanry, up at the Drill Hall on the edge of the park. The ten blasts on the hooter was not only to tell everyone about England going to war, they were also the signal for the Swindon Squadron to make their way to the station in Old Town, straight away. With him gone, it were agreed that Auntie Jean would move back to her sister's the very next day.

'So, we'll have a free bed in the house,' Mam carried on. 'And I've talked over with Father what's to happen about that.'

I feeled myself getting more an more excited. Birdy and the fear of the tunnel an Jim not talking to me was all gone out of my head.

'And we've decided to give it up for some other volunteers.'

She looked at Dad and nodded, and he nodded back. I looked from one to the other, then at Jim. I didn't understand what she meant. Other volunteers. What other volunteers? What were she talking about? That was my bed. Jim an me had shared a bed for the last few years, top-to-tail. We was too big now. It were time for me to have one of my own, and him of course. I tried to speak, to ask what Mam meant. But Dad talked at the same time, in his usual loud voice, not hearing me at all.

'Lord Kitchener has asked for volunteers to go an fight the Hun,' he says. 'And tomorrow, trainloads of them men will start coming into Town and need places to stay before they head off to their training camps.'

I tried again to say something, but Mam held up her hand and shook it like she was holding a little bell. I knowed what that meaned. With the Boiler Shop being so loud, Dad and the other men used signals to talk to each other. Dad brought them signals home with him and 'cause of his deafness we all used them round the house. The little bell signal meaned the foreman was speaking, and everybody else had to shut up an listen.

'If either of you went off to war,' Mam said, pointing at me an Jim. 'I know how I'd feel about a family taking you in an giving you bed an board. It's the least we can do for these brave souls.'

'So, tomorrow,' Dad carries on. 'We're to be

sharing our home with four brand new soldiers.'

He looks at Mam an smiles.

'And they'll all be wearing dresses.'

4. THE CHERRY TREE

Four? How could there be four new people in the house. There weren't barely room for us as it was, even with Uncle Phil an Auntie Jean gone. But four more! And wearing dresses an all. Why would that Lord Kitchener need a load of women in his army? It didn't make no sense. It weren't no clearer when they turned up neither. They wasn't women at all, but lads aged about eighteen or nineteen what filled the front room just by standing there. Jim got on with them straight off, like old pals.

In the end, it turns out they was from Scotland, and the stuff about dresses was just Dad's idea of a joke, 'cause of kilts. It weren't a very funny joke though.

Two of the volunteers slept in the front room on foldaway beds the army buyed from McKilroy's, the big department store in Town. Another of 'em had one of them beds in our room, and the last was on Uncle Phil and Auntie Jean's bed, that I thought should be mine.

Mam fussed around them the whole time like the rest of us was invisible. They didn't have kilts neither, just normal clothes like the rest of us. They weren't to get their uniforms until they got to training camp, which were a week later. Which meaned another week before I got a bed of my own. Another week squeezed in next to Jim. And just to make it about as bad as possible, the other two lads had our room, so Jim and me had to move our bed into Mam an Dad's room. At nights I couldn't sleep at all, with the stink of Jim's feet, an Dad snoring like a steam hammer on the other side of the room. And Mam's chest wheezing in an out an all.

On Sunday, we went to church together, and the Scots met up with all their mates who was there with their families. Even through mass they chatted to each other and smoked cigarettes. I could tell the Reverend weren't happy, but he didn't say nothing. After the service were over, I took myself off and sat in the cemetery up on the hill.

I had a secret bench next to the path what runs through the graves, under a wild cherry tree. It were quiet there, with all them dead folk sleeping all peaceful like, and it was good for just sitting and thinking. Some times I'd take one of Jim's engineering books with me, but only the ones with lots of pictures. Most days I just sat an looked out over the railway works.

Them workshops stretched on for miles it seemed. Long brick walls with piers and arches, and the slopes of their roofs jagging up and down like some giant saw blade. All around, there was tracks going in every direction and the locomotives heaving an pumping out their steamy smoke. On most days I could hear the noises from the works an all, especially the Boiler Shop, with all them hammers echoing inside the metal. In the summer heat, that sound was like a thunderstorm coming in. Or maybe the sound of them big guns over in France, booming and killing everything in their way. On Sundays though, it were silent.

'Penny for 'em,' a voice says to me, in a funny accent.

Blinking from the sun, I turned to see it were one of the Scottish volunteers from our house. He were hovering like he wanted to sit on the bench but was waiting for me to say it was alright. I turned back to the view and grunted some, which he took as me agreeing, even though that weren't how I meaned it at all.

'Best time of year to sit under one of these,' he says, as he sat down next to me.

I looked at him, but he were looking straight ahead.

'In a few weeks, all the leaves will turn red and start falling off. Then through the winter, the deadwood will break off. Spring, there'll be a short spell where it'll look glorious in its blossom. That will all drop off too, and the fruit'll come and the birds will peck away most of it and throw cherry stones all over the place. And any they don't get will end up covering your bench in sticky red goo.'

He turned to me, and I just gawped at him.

'But right now,' he says, twisting his body so he's facing me more. 'For these few summer weeks, a wild cherry tree is just lovely green leaves and nothing falls on your head at all. Best time to sit under it.'

He smiled and looked me straight in the eye. I felt my body relax some, an even a small smile coming on to my face.

'Edward. Edward Macpherson,' he says, and thrust his hand out.

I shaked it, and he chatted away some more. He was probably a bit taller than me, and thinnish like me, an his accent weren't quite as strong as the other three Scots staying with us. Which meaned I could understand everything he said. His hair was black as soot, greased back off a high, pale forehead, an his chin looked like it were in shadow even though it was clean shaven. And I hadn't even noticed before that he were wearing glasses. Small round ones. Truth is, I hadn't really noticed anything about any of the Scots since they'd arrived, except that they was taking over the whole house and Mam were giving them all our food.

'You don't look like a soldier,' I says after a bit.

'That's because I'm not,' he told me. 'I'm a scholar, at Glasgow University. Studying botany. At least I was, until this blessed war broke out and we all decided to do our bit. But I'm sure it'll be an adventure. And it'll all be over by Christmas, and I can get back to my studies.'

'What's it's like?' I asked. 'Studying, I mean.'

He pulled his chin back some and his eyebrows lifted some, looking at me like I were a bit mad. I felt all embarrassed all of a sudden, my face flushing up. But he shook his head, and waved a hand.

'Oh, sorry,' he says. 'Didn't mean to look so surprised. It's just that, well, I figured you lads all went into the works. Into the railways, like your dad and your brother.'

Of course that's what everyone thought. Especially Dad an Jim. And Uncle Phil and Grandma. And the other kids at school and all our neighbours and the shopkeepers and deliverymen, and just about everyone else an all. The railway Company was everything in this town, and it were near impossible to do anything else but end up there. Even if you hated everything about it. The only person who were different was Mam.

'Don't you listen to them,' she'd say to me when it were just me an her together. 'You've got a brain in there, my clever little Noggin. It'd be a sin to just throw that away.'

The masters at school didn't care what she thought, mind. I weren't so good at the things they wanted us to learn. Like reading and writing an that. Though it were different with numbers an stuff. Somehow, I could see number problems dead easy, and could remember everything they told us in science. Mam reckoned that were proof I was smart. The masters just said that made me perfect for working on the railways. But Mam knowed I hated them railway works. She knew why an all. So did Dad an Jim, but they never spoke of it. Nobody did any more. And I weren't about to blurt it out to someone I hardly knowed, like a volunteer soldier with a funny accent. I perched on the edge of the bench and stared at the works. Then I did blurt something out. I said something to Edward Macpherson what I'd never said out loud before, to no-one, never.

'I ain't going to work there,' I says, in not much more than a whisper. 'Not ever. I'm going to get me a proper education and use the brains God gave me.'

I pursed my lips and nodded, an quickly twisted to look at Edward. To make sure he weren't laughing at me, or disapproving none. His face was dead set. He gived a little nod himself, and leaned towards me an patted me on the shoulder.

'Good for you, Noggin,' he says. 'You stand up for yourself.'

Then he says something else, an my mouth dropped open.

'After all, with your dad and Jim joining up to fight the Hun, you'll soon be the man of the house, and it'll be your word that counts.'

5. JOINING UP

I walked the long way round to the Pattern Store, where the motor lorries was. And my leg behaved itself all the way. Hardly any pain an no stiffness. A good leg day.

It were a risk, of course, going on a works lorry, but I didn't have no choice. Besides, I didn't care none anyway. That Scotsman, Edward Macpherson, was right. My father and my brother had made a decision that they was going to join the army. To fight in the war. Without a single word to me. Their son, their younger brother. Even strangers knowed before I did. Well, if that was how it was to be, then I'd make a decision of my own, an I wouldn't say a word to them neither.

Of course, I didn't just decide it like that. It took a long time and a lot of thinking. Mam was right about them changes though. It were all different at home for them days, and not just 'cause of Edward Macpherson and the other volunteers neither. In fact, after our talking under the cherry tree, I realised them was all nice blokes, but especially Edward, and I stopped minding about not getting a bed of my own an that. Edward did everything to help around the house, even giving Mam a hand with the washing an stuff in the kitchen. Best of all, he put special times aside just to talk to me. I liked listening to his soft accent, and his telling of stories about Scotland and university and trees and flowers. And our talks made me think more about me doing something different than going into the works an that, even though I knowed it would probably never happen. Not really. Dad said Edward talked too much. Posh nonsense, he said, even though he couldn't hear a word of it, and I shouldn't pay no heed.

In the end, that week they was with us went by too quick. We was all sorry when they had to leave. Even Dad said it felt like they'd become proper members of the family. On the day they was to head off to their training camp to join the Cameron Highlanders Regiment I went off to the cemetery and sat under the cherry tree. That were a bad leg day and it took me a long time to walk up there. I didn't cry though.

It were something else that really helped my decision, mind. Dad and Edward was full of it, going on all the time about the war an the army, with hardly a word to me anymore. After they'd been to a big meeting at the Mechanics' Institution, with all the other men and apprentices from the works, it were like they forgot me altogether. All they could think about was joining up, talking to each other about it all the time, Dad in his loud voice.

'We all has to make sacrifices, son,' I hear Dad say to Jim one evening. 'And until the war's over, I'm afraid you just have to forget about your apprenticeship in the works.'

I couldn't believe it. Going to war meant not going into the works. I didn't show no-one what that made me think of, or how it made me feel, but it made my mind up for me, good an proper.

A big crowd of men was already there when I comed under the bridge on the Rodbourne Road, and there was three motor lorries. I held back and watched while a locomotive rumbled over the ironworks above the road. Dad an Jim was there, and Birdy an all, which were a surprise to me. With his crafty ways, and with him being so skinny an that, I never even thought about him joining up. Even from my hiding place I could see the bruises on his face.

I watched, and seed 'em all climb into one of the lorries with about thirty or more others. As the lorry growled and set off towards me, I pulled my flat cap down to hide my face. In case they looked my way. Then I went an joined the queue what was left, keeping my head down until I were in a lorry. My heart skipped a beat when I seed William Adams sitting there an all. But if he seed me, he weren't about to show it. His green eyes was flat an staring ahead, never looking at anyone else. I knowed why an all. Nothing to do with me an Jim an Birdy. It was his own dad's fault.

Mr Adams was in the works an all, in a different department from his son. But no-one talked to him, not ever, on account of something he done years back. From what Jim told me, there were an accident when a boiler blowed up, an a bunch of men got killed. Adams' dad was on the team what had riveted the boiler, but he went straight off to management an reported the rest of the team, making out it were their fault. His mates. They all got sacked except him. No-one had talked to him since, and they didn't like his son 'cause of it neither. That was why William Adams kept his mouth shut when he was with other men from the works. Maybe that were why he was going off same as me, to join Kitchener's army.

*

Devizes don't look like Devizes anymore. You couldn't see the houses for the people and the flags hanging out. And the streets was busy with soldiers, marching and doing all that soldiers do, and folk who's there to be soldiers and people come to see 'em.

The only place there was space to walk was on the roads, in the dried out mud along with the horses and the heat from the sun and the motor lorries, and the horse shit. I was jostled by carts going this way and that, and by great long lines of soldiers marching down the streets as far as you can see. There was horses pulling gun carriages an all, only they didn't have no guns on 'em. And then there was loads of other men an lads, more than you know was alive, all pushing their way into town, same as me.

I tried to get on the pavement, where I could see the shops and know where I was. But every time I got on, I just got squeezed off again. It were hard to get my bearings. Couldn't see nothing but men's backs or horses legs. I wiped sweat off my face and shouted at the people what shoved me, but it were pointless. What with all the chatter and other shouting and the clip clop of horses and the engines and the hooters on the lorries, even I couldn't hear me when I shouted out. And there was a great brass band an all, full of men in red tunics and instruments shining like silver in the summer sunshine. Blowing out music that makes your chest insides tingle.

I'd been to Devizes a dozen times or more, but I might as well as been in a different place altogether for all I knew where I really was. Proper lost. There were only one thing to do. Go in the same direction as the others an hope it would get me somewhere.

And it did. After a bit I passed through the town centre and found where they was making the new army. What they called the recruiting grounds.

'Bloody Mary,' I swears, after making sure there weren't no-one there what knowed me.

I never seen so many men all in one place. Over one way was the big army building, what I knowed was the Devizes barracks. All red brick and looking like a castle, with its battlements and two big towers. Of course I'd seen that before, but it did look different now. All the land around was filled right up with rows of white tents. And each one had a queue of men sticking out of 'em that must've been a mile long. I took a breath. Then, bold as brass, I walked up an stood myself at the end of one of them queues, right next to a post which had a picture of a man nailed to it. He had a big moustache like Dad's and a smart hat. I knowed it was Lord Kitchener, and it said stuff along the bottom. I could read *God Save the King*.

As I shuffled along with everyone else, the queue never seemed to get any shorter. The more I had to wait, the more nervy I got. On the outside I hoped I just looked like every other body. Just another person in the queue, waiting for his turn. But inside, it were a different story. My tummy was fit to burst, the gurgling were so awful. Sweat trickling down inside my shirt and trousers. In my head, the thinking were too fast for me to make any sense of it. They was all in there, voices telling me what to do, all arguing and saying how it should be.

'We's all very proud of you, son,' says Dad's voice. 'Fighting for your country. You're a real man now.' Then he says, 'How dare you sign up without my permission, you evil little boy, now who will look after your mother?' And, 'Why would they want a stupid little cripple like you?'

And Mam joins in an all. But she is mostly just crying and screaming an I can't hear what she's saying. And Jim too. One minute he is patting me on the back, then next he's lost it and shouting at me and giving me a hiding.

Then I hears the recruiting soldier's voice loud an clear, sitting at his table in the tent.

'Age,' I hear him asking the man at the front.

My heart jumped. Of course I knowed I was under the age you needed to be to join up. But in all my thinking, I figured I could easily fool 'em I was older. I didn't have Jim's size, of course, but I were still from the same good engineering stock, after all. I looked around me. I weren't the biggest, that's for sure. But I weren't the smallest neither. In with the normal size men, there was plenty of scrawny looking lads. Maybe country boys, like Birdy. If they could get in, then so could I, I reckoned.

Even so, now I were close, I weren't that sure.

Then before I knowed it, I was stood in front of the table telling the soldier everything he wants to know, the dates and numbers an that came into my head without even thinking. The man filled in his bit of paper and shoved it at me and told me to go into the tent. And all through it, he don't even bat an eyelid or even really look at me like I was there at all.

Inside the tent I waited to be medical checked. And I was smiling. Even though I telled a lie, a big lie, I couldn't help the grin growing across my face. My skin was tingling. And all I wanted to do was talk, or maybe even sing. The inside of the tent were like a stove, full of the hot air of thousands of men going through and the sun beating down on it all day. But even though the sweat was pouring off me, I didn't care.

I had to strip off some, and them men called Medical Orderlies, with their white coats, measured me and prodded me and asked me lots of questions. They said I was tall enough and my chest was big enough. Just. It made me stand up straighter and stick out my chest a little bit more. Then one of them asked me if I had any medical ailments.

6. MARCHING

Marching was what the army cared about most, I reckon. No-one was bothered if I had anything wrong with my leg or nothing, not really. Just so long as I could march. Or do drill, as they called it. As it happens, it weren't my leg that were the problem anyway. It were my shoes.

Me an Jim an Birdy got letters saying we had to report on Salisbury Plain. Dad got a different letter, telling him he couldn't join up. His deafness would be a danger to him and every other soldier, they told him.

On the day we had to go, I weren't able to find my letter anywhere, and we was supposed to take 'em with us. I had to search high an low. Luckily I found it just as Birdy and his dad turned up. It were behind the curtain in the front room.

Then Birdy's dad took us in his cart with some

others from Town. Mam ran back in the house, coughing and crying. Dad held me back when I went to follow, jut giving a little shake of his head. He looked like he might cry himself. I wanted to think that was 'cause he were sad we was going, like Mam, or dead proud of us an that. He might've had some of them thoughts about Jim, but mostly I reckon he was upset on account of not being allowed to go himself.

As the cart pulled away he holded up both fists in front of his chest, and pumped 'em towards us. Me an Jim both knowed what it meaned. In the works that were the foreman's signal to the rivet gun team. Everyone's in place. Everything's set. Go.

When we got down to the Plain, we just had to queue up outside a tent again. It took nearly the whole day. Then we was put in a group of about a dozen or so and taken to a different tent by a man called Corporal Simpson. He told us we was called 2 Section, an he were our Section Leader. He were old, older than dad at least, and fat, and muttered to himself the whole time. And even though he were wearing a uniform, it looked even older than him, an there weren't no chance of the buttons being done up round that big gut. The tent he took us to were in a great long row of tents, with a thousand other rows. Full of lads who'd gone an joined Kitchener's army. Millions of us, it felt like. But I didn't see no sign of

Adams. Maybe he didn't make it.

In the tent there was a small oil stove when you first go in, and a row of beds down each side. Each bed had a folded up blanket on it, and a mess tin for eating out of, and a shovel. There weren't much else. I did get to have a bed all of my own at last, though. But it weren't what I hoped for. Not at all.

'You sleep down that end of the tent,' Jim says to me when we got there. 'We don't want you with us.'

I stood there looking at him, half hoping he'd change his mind. But he weren't about to. He turned his back and him an Birdy chatted to each other.

Down the far end of the tent I found a spare bed next to a tiny bloke who's skin was almost white, it were so pale. And deep dark hollows around his eyes. It were a wonder to me that he got into the army at all. Right from the off, everyone called him Sadsack. He didn't seem to mind though. Opposite us, Corporal Simpson had his bed and he had a cupboard an all, and a little paraffin burner for heating his own tea.

The blanket on my bed were thin and scratched at my skin, leaving me half shaking cold, half sweating hot on that first night. It weren't a proper bed neither, just a canvas on a metal frame over the bare chalk earth. I used my folded jacket as a pillow, and Jim an Birdy seemed a million miles away down the other end, with all them others between me an them.

I never knowed Jim to be like that with me before.

Dad and Mam was livid, of course, when they found out I'd joined up. Dad shouted at me over an over, and even whacked me when I first told 'em. He were doubly angry on account of him not being allowed to go, I reckon. Mam stomped around the house, doing her chores, snapping at everyone and arguing with Dad about me being too young and saying he should ruddy well do something about it. But in the end there weren't nothing to be done. Dad said we'd get in more trouble if the army knowed I'd lied to 'em. Besides, he reckoned it wouldn't be long before they seed I were a cripple an sent me home again anyhow.

The worst of it though, were Jim. He didn't fly into one of his tempers like I thought he would. Instead, he just paid me no attention at all, only speaking when he really had to. He wouldn't even look at me, and turned his back whenever he seed me. I wished he'd just shout an scream, or even give me a good beating, if it'd just mean he'd talk to me again, proper like.

I feeled like I spent the whole night just trying to get comfortable in that army bed, listening to everyone else snoring, and breathing in the stink of sweat and hair oil, and them others farting. But I must've fallen asleep, 'cause next thing I knowed Corporal Simpson were shouting right in my ear.

'On parade,' he hollers. 'Ten minutes. Up you get you young scally!'

I turned over and seed his round face, with its big red nose, grinning at me. I sat up and rubbed my eyes. He were already dressed in his badly fitting uniform an worked his way round the tent, making sure everyone else was getting up.

'What about breakfast?' I heared Birdy ask. 'Don't we get any breakfast?'

'Parade first, young man,' Corporal Simpson says, leaving the tent. 'Come on. No dilly-dallying.'

One or two of the other lads got up and did their shaving, standing there in just their pants an vest an that. I reached out and pulled on my shirt, then my trousers, using the blanket to keep me private as it were. I already had my socks on, hadn't taken 'em off. Of course, we didn't have no uniforms yet. Some had joined up wearing their Sunday best. Smart jackets and ties an everything. Me an Jim comed in working clothes, on account of Mam saying we'd be getting uniforms anyways, so we should leave our best at home, for when the war was over.

When I were dressed, I reached under the bed for my shoes. At first, I couldn't feel 'em where I thought they was, so I leaned down to get a better look. But I still couldn't see 'em. I were confused, an looked round at everyone else. They was all just getting ready, some of 'em near fully dressed an looking like they was going to set off. I dropped onto my knees and swinged my arm under the bed. Still nothing.

'Come on, you lot,' shouted one of the other lads. 'Sooner this bleedin' parade is over, sooner we get a cup of tea.'

'And breakfast,' says Birdy.

I could feel my heart starting to beat faster. I lifted up the blanket and stuck my head right down on the floor. There weren't no two ways about it, my shoes wasn't there. I jumped up and looked all around the bed, tugging the blanket an that off altogether. The blokes either side of me was done, an headed off. Even Sadsack. At the other end of the tent, I seed Jim head out after Birdy. I were just about to shout out after him, but I weren't quick enough, an he were gone. Besides, he probably wouldn't have taken no notice of me anyhow.

Soon, there was just me left. I sat down on the edge of the bed, clutching the blanket on my lap. Then the Corporal appeared again, sticking his head through the tent flap.

'Up you jump lad,' he said. 'Parade won't start until everyone's present and correct.'

Then he was gone again. And I knowed I had no

choice but to follow him, in my socks.

Outside, there was men all over, lining up in big groups with other men shouting at 'em. More an more was still pouring out of the tents. It was sunny, and the chalky soil of Salisbury Plain were hard under my feet.

I spotted our group, 2 Section, straight off on account of Jim standing taller than most, and made my way towards 'em, hoping no one would notice I didn't have no shoes. If I were lucky, this parade thing would be over real quick, like the lads said, and I could sneak off and find 'em during breakfast. I must've just put 'em somewhere stupid.

'Don't dilly-dally lad,' said Corporal Simpson, trotting past me as he tried to organise everyone, an wheezing with the effort.

I tried to get in close to Jim an Birdy, but the line closed up just as I got near and I had to stand further along. But at least that meaned I weren't near the front, so my feet was good an hid.

Everyone hustled around me, and prattled on to each other like a bunch of starlings. Then whistles blasted out, and men in proper uniforms comes strutting around us.

'Silence in the ranks,' they yelled. 'Silence!'

Bit by bit the noise died down, and our Corporal and others shifted everyone. We was moved to be with three other Sections, to make up what they called a platoon. 4 Platoon. And we all had to stick our arms out, first in front, then to our sides, an shuffle about until we was the right distance from each other. Then we just had to stand there an wait some.

'For crying out loud,' I heared Birdy muttering. 'Ain't we never going to get any breakfast?'

The answer came from a man with three stripes on his arm and a big moustache. He appeared right behind where Birdy was standing.

'No you bleedin' ain't,' the man says, marching to the front of our group and turning to face us all. 'What d'you think this is? A bleedin' picnic? Now stand up straight, you lazy load of beggars. You're in His Majesty's British Army now!'

The man said he was our Platoon Sergeant, Sergeant Hodson, and we was to call him Staff.

'And the first thing we learns in His Majesty's British Army,' he carries on. 'Is how to march like proper bleedin' soldiers.'

My heart sank.

The thought of marching with my rotten leg were bad enough. But with no shoes, I didn't know what I were going to do. I started to put my hand up, like I were at school wanting to go to the toilet. But the Sergeant was already turning away, and something catched my eye. For a moment I forgot about my own feet an squinted at him. I could've sworn I seed him limp.

7. ARMY LIFE

'When I says so, you swing your left leg an your right arm, and then you swing your right leg an your left arm. And I do mean swing. Left, right, left right.'

The Sergeant's words didn't sink in at all. Left, right. Right, left, right. My eyes was all over the place, looking to Jim, an anyone else, hoping for someone to tell me what to do about my shoes. I tried to get Corporal Simpson's attention, but he just shushed me and waved for me to turn back to Sergeant Hodson.

'Right, you miserable lot,' the Sergeant shouts. '4 Platoon. By the left. Quick march!'

Everyone else seemed to get it straight off, and strided out. Leaving me behind. And if the Sergeant did limp before, there weren't no sign of it as he marched. Legs straight as rods. I tried to do the same, but before we even got hardly any distance at all we stopped again, all of a sudden like. Sergeant Hodson had his hand up to stop us, and were staring upwards.

'What the bleedin' 'eck...?' he says.

Everyone looked up. Me an all. There was a flagpole there, just ahead of us. But it weren't no British flag hanging from it. It took a moment for me to twig what I were looking at. But then a hot flush rushed up my neck an over my face. It were my shoes.

'What sort of nonsense is this?' The Sergeant asked, turning back to face us. 'Please tell me that this is nothing to do with any of you lot. God 'elp you if it is.'

I were about three or four yards behind the rest of 'em, with Corporal Simpson next to me. He'd tried to move me on, get me to catch up with the others. It just didn't happen. But not 'cause of my leg, or having no shoes. I'd swinged my legs straight, like the Sergeant done and that weren't too bad for me, just how the doctor telled me I should walk. And the chalky ground was flat and smooth under my socked feet. What really made me mess up, was that I couldn't get my left and right the proper way round. To tell truth, I weren't good with that left an right stuff at any time, but I were trying so hard it all keeped going wrong somehow. My stomach were getting all knotted up with it. Then seeing my shoes hanging there for all of 'em to see was just too much. I could feel my lip trembling. I dropped my head, and stared down at my feet through blurry eyes. My socks was white with the chalk, and all baggy around my ankles.

'Oh goodness me,' says the Corporal, muttering under his breath. 'Goodness, goodness me.'

In a second, Sergeant Hodson's shiny leather boots was there, toe to toe with my shabby feet. I didn't look up. Didn't want to see his face, nor any others. I could feel the eyes of everyone in 2 Section, Jim an Birdy especially, an the other Sections an all. And probably every other person there on the parade ground. All staring at me and my feet. The Sergeant let out a long puff of air through his nose, then he turned away without even saying anything to me at all.

As he went off I heared laughing, real loud like. Then a shout.

'Attention, men,' says the voice. 'All salute the new Company flag!'

I couldn't help but look up. Just a few yards away, in the front row of the Section next to ours, was William Adams.

*

My feet and legs seemed to always be trouble for me. I were only six when my big leg problem first happened. Except it weren't actually my leg what was the problem, not really. It were my back. My spine.

Dad decided one day to take me an Jim into the railway works. It was summer, at the time of the Trip, the big holiday when the works shut down and most folk went away to the seaside. Only we couldn't go that year on account of Mam's coughing getting real bad, and we had to pay for the doctor and medicines an that. But Dad said it were a good chance to show us what it were like in the works, with it being so quiet. He wanted me an Jim to be apprentices one day, then get jobs there, same as him.

I don't remember much about it. Mainly, just how big everything were, and the smells of oil and burnt metal. Them buildings took ages to walk through, even more than walking through Town it seemed, and every thing in there was as big as a house. Furnaces, boilers, cranes, lathes, winches. And the engines and carriages of course. All of 'em huge. Me an Jim 'specially liked climbing through the train wheels. Everyone of 'em was twice as big as me, an bigger than Jim an all in them days. Even bigger than Dad. Dad did tell us not to touch nothing, mind. And telled Jim to keep an eye on me, 'cause it could be dangerous. And even though he were probably right about that, it weren't any of them machines, or the sharp edged tools, or nothing heavy or hard what caused my leg problem. It were a greasy sleeper. That's all.

As we was walking home that day, we crossed the traverser, outside the workshops. Dad told us that when the works was fully up an running, that traverser would be busy all day long, shifting left an right helping engines move in an out of the sheds. But with everyone away on the Trip it were sitting quiet so we took a short cut across its tracks. According to what Mam told me later, I slipped on the oily top of one of them wooden sleepers. When I fell down, something got hurt in my spine.

I don't remember that at all. Nothing about it. The only bit that stayed with me is the remembering of them big sheds, and all the machines. But every time I think of them they is all dark and unfriendly like, and my tummy tightens up something awful. And the worst is at night, when they fill up my head an I can't escape. On account of my bad leg.

Luckily though, after them first few days, my leg seemed to like army life in the main. And I didn't mind it too much neither. Of course I hated it when my shoes was up the flagpole, but afterwards most folk seemed to be that bit kinder to me. Except Adams and Jim. But I figured it were best not to think about that too much. Besides, there was enough else to think about.

Mostly what we did was marching drill, which meaned keeping your legs straight, swinging 'em just like the doctor told me to do. It were hard, and they never let up on us. But I didn't care because every other person had to walk the same as me. It were the first time in my life when I wasn't the odd one out all the time.

Of course I still had bad leg days, but a good stamping usually got me through it. That didn't stop me getting in a muddle with left an right mind. But I weren't alone with that. Some men got sick an all, with loads not fit enough to stand it, and there was all manner of foot problems, boils and blisters an that. No wonder neither. Marching up an down, counter-marching, wheeling left, then right, then left again. And forming squares 'til the cows came home. It were like they didn't know what else to do with us. Too many men, we reckoned, and with all the proper officers and sergeants already out fighting the Hun, them what was left behind had their hands full trying to sort things.

Luckily, our uniforms did turn up, at least most of the stuff. Shirts, underwear and of course real army trousers an tunic. They was made of rough serge in a dirty greeny brown colour, an so was the cap comforter, which were good for keeping your head warm. We got puttees an all. Long strips of cloth which we was supposed to wrap round our legs to keep water out of the boots. Except there weren't no boots yet, so I were stuck with my shabby old shoes. Even so, we was glad of what we did get, especially when autumn turned to winter proper. Me an Jim's clothes was almost turned to rags by then and the wind on the Plain were like ice blowing through you.

Even our new uniforms couldn't keep that cold out, but at least we feeled more like soldiers.

No guns, mind. Instead, we had to do our marching carrying dummy guns, made of wood, which we all hated. Especially Birdy. He couldn't wait to get his hands on a real gun. And we weren't so lucky with food, neither. There weren't no breakfast most of them days, and the other food we got was usually horrible. Watery Machonochie soup, with tiny bits of turnip, carrot and potato what tasted of tin can, or bully beef and dry bread or biscuits hard as steel, if we was lucky. And never enough of it, an no milk or sugar for tea. Though at least the tea were hot, mostly.

If we wasn't drilling or thinking about food, then they made up things for us to do. Like sitting in our tent and cleaning our mess tins with bath blocks.

'This is just plain stupid,' says Jim, trying to rub the big block of clay into the corners of his tin.

He weren't talking to me, mind. He was still angry

it seemed, with me an the tunnel, or for joining up, or whatever it was. The only time he talked to me was when we got a letter from home. Dad writed to us every week in his curly writing, and Jim telled me what he said, then writed back an telled what we was doing. On account of me not being so good with all that reading an writing an stuff. I didn't mind too much. At least it meaned I got to have my brother talking to me some.

8. MY FIRST OFFICER

A head stuck through our tent flap, and shouted in.

'Footie!'

The message were simple, and everyone stopped what they was doing an looked at each other.

'What we waiting for?' Says one bloke, jumping up from his bed an heading towards the flap. 'Anyone coming?'

The others mostly started up from their bunks an all, and I seed Jim and Birdy look at each other. They grinned, shrugged and then they jumped up too, and followed the rest out of the tent. I were a bit surprised at Jim. I knowed the apprentices back at the works had footie matches on Faringdon Park of a lunchtime, but Jim always says he couldn't be bothered with that sort of thing. Rather read his engineering books, or just carry on working. But I suppose anything were better than sitting there in the cold trying to polish a mess tin with a lump of bath block. Even to Jim.

Me an Sadsack was left sitting on our beds. There weren't no point in me going out, nor him. Neither of us was any good for football, and I knowed them others wouldn't want us on their teams. That was for sure. I didn't say nothing, and turned back to my tin.

'We could go an watch,' Sadsack says.

I had the same idea, but I were nervous in case someone tried to make me play.

'Or we could get something to eat,' he says.

That made me stop an look up at him. His pale, pointy face was staring, his eyes big lost in them dark shadows.

'What're you on about?' I asked. 'What food?'

'You won't like it.'

'Eh? What d'you mean? Do you know where there's some food or not?'

'I think so. But I don't think you'll like it.'

'For Goodness' sake, Sadsack,' I says, dumping the bath block down on my bed. 'Just tell me.'

So he did, and he were right, I didn't like it. Well, it weren't so much that I didn't like it, it just sounded stupid, and revolting an all. Snails. Sadsack's idea was we go looking for snails, an he wouldn't give up on it. He reckoned he'd heard tell of some men who'd gone collecting snails. Then, when the snails was fished out of their shells and boiled up with lots of salt an pepper, they was alright. Like mussels or cockles or something like that.

'We could get enough for everyone,' he added. 'Have a proper meal ready for when they come back.'

I weren't sure about it. Not for a second. But I couldn't see too much harm in giving it a try.

'You'll have to taste 'em first,' I says, getting my shoes on.

I wish I hadn't bothered.

'What in God's name is that smell?' Jim says as he comes back into the tent after the footie.

The others came in an all, sweating an shouting about who did good an who scored an that. It sounded like Jim done real well. From what they was saying, Jim's size an strength made him near impossible to tackle, even for wiry William Adams, who were on the other team. The losers. Jim even scored a goal an all. But the excited talking all stopped as the whiff hit the lads' nostrils, an their faces scrunched up. They all grabbed at their noses and sweared. As they pushed their way in, I let them shove me back, further away from the stove. I was thinking maybe they wouldn't reckon the stink were anything to do with me.

'It's okay,' shouts Sadsack, standing there next to the stove waving his arms. 'It's food for everyone. Me an Noggin done it.'

'God,' says Birdy. 'Look at what they've done to our kettle pan. Urgh, that's disgusting.'

He showed the pan round to some of the others, holding it at arm's length and pulling the sourest face ever. Everyone else made noises like they was spewing up and turned away, waving their hands to get rid of the smell or pulling shirts over their faces. Birdy went off out of the tent. When he came back a moment later, the pan were empty, and he threw it at me.

'You'd better hope our tea don't taste of that shit,' he says, looking to me an then at Sadsack. 'Clean it proper, both of you.'

The others gathered around the stove. I seed Jim looking at me. He didn't say nothing. He didn't need to.

'Come on Birdy,' one bloke shouted. 'We've got the victor's spoils to enjoy!'

'Yeah,' says Birdy, joining 'em and slapping Jim on the back. 'Stick that in your pipe and smoke it, William Adams.'

Sadsack and me headed down our end of the tent, and looked at each other. I sat on my bunk an shaked my head at him, then picked up my bath brick. Couldn't believe I'd been so stupid. I felt a flush coming over my face, an wished I could just run away. Go and sit in the cemetery under my cherry tree. I thought about what I said to Edward Macpherson about getting proper educated. How could I even think I could ever be clever. So stupid.

The others all carried on with their footie shouting, then they all give out a huge cheer what made me an Sadsack look up.

'What they got, Nicholas?' Asked Sadsack.

I swinged round and glared at him.

'Don't call me that,' I says. 'My name's Noggin.'

I turned an stretched my neck up as long as I were able, trying to see.

A can. They had a big tin can of something, and it were soon open and sitting on the stove. I couldn't see what were in it, but I didn't need to. Soon enough, the smell telled me exactly what it was. Treacle pudding. A whole can of delicious, soft, sticky treacle pudding. Steaming hot. I flopped back down and gawped. My mouth was dribbling. I couldn't help it, an wiped my lips with the back of my sleeve. Then I seed there weren't just one tin, but a load of 'em, maybe a dozen. I don't know what was in them others, but it were no wonder they was all cheering. What a prize for winning a footie match. Except the noise stopped, all of a sudden.

The crowd moved aside, and I seed there was three men coming into the tent. It were Sergeant Hodson.

And with him was a policeman, a regular bobby, and a soldier carrying a rifle. They ignored Jim an Birdy and the rest, and came straight down the tent towards me.

'Private Arkell?' The Sergeant asked, his moustache twitching. 'Private Nicholas Arkell?'

I stayed just where I was, and nodded, staring wide-eyed at the men standing over me.

There weren't no talking after that. Sergeant Hodson led off and I had to follow, with the policemen next to me and the soldier with his gun right behind. Straight to the Barracks, having to march real fast past all the tents, with everyone looking as we went past. Including Adams, who sneered at me with them green eyes sparkling as I got taked off towards the old castle building.

'So is it true?' The policeman says to me, as we waits outside the Commanding Officer's room.

I looked to Sergeant Hodson, but didn't know what to say. Didn't know what he were talking about.

'Answer the constable, lad,' says the Sergeant.

I stared at the policeman. He had a red face and white eyebrows, and was staring right back at me. I turned my eyes away, and looked down the red brick corridor, trying to think of what to say. After a moment he huffs at me, and pulls out a piece of paper from his pocket an unfolds it.

'Well, boy? How old are you?' He says, waving the paper at me. 'Is this true?'

At first the man's question didn't sink in proper. Standing there in that dark, cool building with its shiny wooden floors and notices stuck up on all the walls, my mind went a bit blurry. But then I twigged what he wanted to know.

'When were you born?' The constable snaps. 'I haven't got all day.'

The answer blurted out. The lie. The same lie I told to the recruiting soldier, about what year I was born. I didn't have no choice. I thinked about what Dad said, about me being in more trouble if they knowed I'd lied. About maybe him and Mam getting into trouble an all. I wanted to explain, to tell the truth. Really I did, but I weren't able to stop myself.

'He looks perfectly old enough to me,' the Sergeant says. 'The lad's nearly as tall as you are, damn it.'

That were true an all. Without his helmet on, the policeman weren't much above my height. I stood up even straighter.

'Can't help that, Sergeant,' the bobby says, tapping the piece of paper with his finger. 'If a law's been broken, it's my duty to bring the guilty to book.'

Sergeant Hodson takes the paper and looks. He sighs, then I seed his eyebrows shifting, and he slowly looks up again, tapping the paper with his

62

forefinger same as the constable had.

'It says Private James Arkell here too,' he says. 'I thought this was supposed to be Nicholas Arkell. You ain't got me here on some sort of foul up have you?'

'Not sure about that,' the constable answers. 'Just know what it says on there about Nicholas Arkell.'

He reached out, snatching the paper back an folding it up again. I tried to say something, to explain about me an Jim being brothers, but the Sergeant speaked over me.

'Come on, lad,' he says, poking me in the chest. 'Best tell us straight. It'll be all the worse for you if you don't give the Major the truth. He ain't one for any nonsense.'

At that moment, the office door flew open and there he was. Our Commanding Officer, Major Cromwell. Right behind him was another officer, Captain Roberts, his Second-in-Command.

I never seen an officer before, not really, and didn't know what to expect. I couldn't believe how smart they was. And it weren't just how the uniforms were, with them perfect fitted tunics and peaked caps, all with neat edging and shiny, shiny buttons, an piping an that on their sleeves. But they were so clean. It looked like them an their uniforms just come straight out the steamer. Their leather belts and boots was so smooth, they looked like polished brown glass. The Sergeant stood to attention, sharp as you like, an snapped his hand up to the side of his head to salute. I tried to copy. Only it weren't quite the same.

The Major waved his hand towards his peak and strutted off, ignoring us completely.

'Ah, Sergeant. Good,' the Captain says, adjusting his cap on his head, making him even smarter. 'This way. And bring those men with you.'

His boots cracked against the tiled floor, as he strided off past us an down the corridor after the Major. The Sergeant an me both jumped to, ready to follow, an so did the soldier with the gun. The policeman's mouth dropped, and he held up his hand.

'Um, Captain,' he says. 'Excuse me, sir. A minute if you don't mind.'

The Captain stopped and looked back, barely turning.

'What is it?' He says. 'I'm a busy man.'

'I appreciate that, Captain,' the policeman says, walking towards the officer and pointing at me. 'But we've had a very serious report about this soldier, about him being underage. I have a duty to investigate.'

Sticking his hands on his hips, the Captain puffed out of his nose.

'It may have escaped your notice, constable,' he

says. 'But we have a war to fight, and we really don't have time for such petty matters.'

He paused and looked at his watch. A wristwatch, with a metal strap. Then he looked at me, but only for a second.

'He looks perfectly able to me. And right now, we have to attend to possibly the most important thing to happen in this camp since the war started.'

9. PROPER SOLDIERS

Short Magazine Lee Enfield. That were the name they gived to the guns we was to use. S.M.L.E. But everyone called 'em *Smellies*.

They came in wooden crates, in a great column of motor lorries. More trucks than I'd even seen at the works, all lined up outside the barracks with the Major and the Captain an other officers there, and Sergeants an that climbing on to check 'em an shouting orders to everyone else. Sergeant Hodson sent me to tell Corporal Simpson that he was to bring our Section over to help unload, and he were to tell the other Sections' Leaders to come an all with their men. The whole of 4 Platoon.

I couldn't believe how heavy them boxes was, nor how heavy one gun was when we got ours issued from the Quartermaster. Our very own gun. One for each of us, with a webbing strap and oil an cleaning kit.

'Nice metalwork,' says Jim, looking his up an down. 'Good British engineering.'

'Bolt action,' says Birdy, holding his up to his shoulder and looking down the sights. '.303 inch calibre, and a ten round magazine.'

He lowered the weapon an looked at the rest of us, his eyes shining.

'That's twice as many bullets as the Huns have in theirs,' he carries on. 'They don't stand a chance when we gets out to France.'

Of course I were as excited about having a gun as Jim an Birdy was, with my own number engraved into the little disc in the butt. But I was nervous an all. About firing it. I couldn't imagine what it would be like. Birdy didn't help much. He kept going on about shooting an guns an that, about how it would jump an bash into your shoulder if you didn't do it right, or maybe blow up in your face if a round got jammed in the breach. But we didn't do no shooting. First we had to learn all about the gun. Stripping it down and loading the magazine. And cleaning it. Then cleaning it again.

'A dirty gun is more likely to kill you than the enemy,' Sergeant Hodson told us. 'And what's the first thing you do when you're cleaning your gun?'

'Make sure it's *your* gun, Staff,' we all says back.

There weren't much chance of us killing ourselves

though, nor no-one else neither. Even after we'd had them Smellies for weeks, we still didn't do no shooting. All we done was drill with 'em. And the weight of that gun weren't good for drilling. When I slinged it over my shoulder it were like having Birdy sitting on there. When we was marching then I felt like Jim was on there an all. And it got worse.

'Right, you lot,' says the Sergeant on parade. 'Being nearly Christmas, I've got presents for you all.'

By then we knowed the Sergeant well enough to know they wouldn't be real presents, an we was right. The rest of our kit had arrived, and we was to head off to the Quartermaster's Stores to collect it.

'And when you've got it all sorted,' the Sergeant carried on, rubbing his gloved hands together. 'Then we can have some proper drill. You'll be headed across to Basingstoke soon, so we need to turn you into real soldiers before then. Full Marching Order.'

Of course none of us had a clue what that meaned. But Corporal Simpson soon showed us.

We was like a bunch of starlings back at the tent, gabbling away as we laid out all our new stuff, all smelling of grease paper and freshness. For a start, there was two haversacks. One small one, which was to contain rations an that. And one big one, a back pack, what came with webbing straps, an a belt with ammunition pouches. We had to buckle 'em all together so you could put everything on or take it all off in one go. Me and Sadsack helped each other work it all out. Actually, I worked it out an helped Sadsack. I were better off doing mine on my own.

Off the belt round your middle hanged a water bottle and an entrenching tool. The wooden handle hanged down one side and the metal digging bit hanged on its own down the back. They all had their own carrying holders. On top of all that we got a rubberised groundsheet, a big thick greatcoat, an a bayonet as long as my arm. And, of course, boots. Real leather, brand new ones that was as solid as you like, an a tin of polish and brushes to go with 'em.

The whole lot was made so well that it felt dead comfy when it was on. Even the boots at first. Until the Corporal told us what was to happen next.

'Right, lads,' he says. 'Pack your spares, your greatcoat and groundsheet into your pack, with your mess tin, polish, shaving kit, and blanket. Fill up your water bottle, then we're off to find some stones. No dilly-dallying.'

At first we was still giggling and talking all excited like, striding off in our shiny boots and with our new packs an webbing an that. We feeled like real soldiers. But then we had to pick up stones, lumps of chalk an flints, an fill all our ammunition pouches to make 'em feel like they was full of bullets. By the time we got back on parade, with our Smellies on our shoulders an all, I feeled like a baggage wagon. And them boots was already starting to rub against my ankles.

It was cold and raining when we got going, an we was all a bit quieter. Almost from the off, I walked lopsided, an my leg cramped up. Stamping it out weren't easy when you's trying to march and carry all that stuff, an get used to new boots an all.

'Watch it, Noggin,' I heared Jim whisper behind me. 'Sergeant's coming.'

I swinged round in surprise. Not just on account of the Sergeant coming though. It was Jim. He'd talked to me. But swinging round was the stupidest thing to do. My bad leg gave way with the sudden movement and I felled out of the ranks and collapsed in a heap on the ground. My gun crashed down next to me, sliding through the wet chalk. Sergeant Hodson turned angry in an instant, like I'd never seen him before.

'What the..,' he shouted, taking huge strides towards me. 'You ruddy little fool. What in Hell's name do you think you're doing?'

He paid no heed to me in the slush, just snatched up the rifle and looks it up and down, cocking it an that. I pulled myself back up, and tried to stand straight. But now my leg had seized altogether. The

Sergeant pushed the gun back at me, and I stumbled backwards, almost falling down again.

'Your most treasured possession. Do you understand me soldier?' He shouted in my face. 'That gun is the most important thing in the world to you!'

Then his head twitched a bit to the side.

'What's wrong with your leg?' He asked, shifting his head, and squinting down at me. 'If I thought you were taking the mickey, soldier...'

Jim appeared by my side.

'That were my fault, Staff,' he said, cutting off the Sergeant an standing to attention. 'I did knock Noggin's, um, Private Arkell's, knee with my gun. Sorry, Staff. Not used to carrying it, that's all.'

Sergeant Hodson looked at Jim, then at me.

'Back in line the pair of you,' he says, wagging his finger at me. 'And if that gun doesn't work, woe betide you Private!'

Then he turned and went off to the head of the column, and I managed to hobble along without him noticing. I wondered what he meaned about taking the mickey. It brought to mind the time I seed him limping. Or thinked I did.

More important than that, though, Jim were talking to me. He was behind me in the ranks. He couldn't see that I were smiling.

*

71

'I hope the food's like this when we gets to France,' says Birdy at breakfast. 'Don't want to be eating them frog legs. Or snails.'

He took a look at me, an winks.

We all loved the canteen hall at Basingstoke. It were like the rest of the camp there. Huge and new. It were right in the middle of row after row of proper-built wooden huts for us to sleep in, and sheds an stables an that, all smelling of fresh timber an varnish. Trucks and horses an soldiers everywhere, even first thing in the morning. Inside the hall made me think of the works, where Dad worked, big as a factory. Hundreds of tables an chairs, thousands maybe, and serving-counters an men queued up outside. All the noise of clanking and talking and eating. Thick, hot porridge, and bacon. Real bacon, an cheese and huge lumps of bread. With a thick layer of something Birdy called axle-grease, which was actually butter, or something like it anyway. Sweet jam an all. Raspberry.

'Sugar,' says Jim, as we sat down at a table. 'There ain't nothing like it.'

He spooned the stuff into his mug of steaming tea and stirred it in with the milk.

I reckon we changed some in them couple of months at Basingstoke, after we leaved Salisbury Plain long behind us. Jim talked to me proper again.

More like we was the same as each other, not him being my big brother all the time. Birdy were nicer an all. And Sadsack even looked a bit more healthy.

Our billet was one of them wooden huts, with about forty or more metal beds, and electric lights an a little cupboard each for keeping our kit and personal bits an pieces. And Jim an Birdy let me have a bed near them. My first proper bed. It made me think the army were proper good.

Reckon all that training was doing what it were supposed to do. Turning us into soldiers. Real soldiers. Even though we never quite got why we had to do so much forced marches and square bashing. And digging ditches and endless cleaning an polishing of stuff. Especially our Smellies.

'Just a shame we can't shoot the things,' Birdy used to say all the time. 'Right bleedin' shame.'

Slope arms. Order arms. Present arms. Trail 'em, pile 'em, three bags full 'em. Everything except fire any real ammo. That were being saved for the Hun they telled us.

Even so, we was starting to realise what it meaned to go to war. What we was going to fight for.

Come Spring, as I seed new leaves starting coming out on the trees, I thinked of Mam, with her coughing. And Dad in his silent world. When orders was posted that we was 'On readiness for Overseas', I realised I weren't yearning for my cherry tree so often. I wanted to get on with it. We was ready.

Corporal Simpson never made it though. Whether he were too fat or too old, or just not up to it, they never told us. One day I came into our billet and his bed was bare. Just a folded grey blanket an his little cupboard empty. No dilly-dallying.

We knowed we was on our way towards France, and the war proper. 'Cause of that we got chits to let us off camp for four days. Me an Jim went home, an so did them others what comed from nearby towns an that. To see our families.

Dad said he were right proud of us, though it were hard to talk to him about any of it. Partly 'cause of his deafness, of course, but also on account of him not paying us too much heed. Just sitting there, staring into nothing mostly. Mam weren't there. Her coughing had got real bad an she'd been taken into the hospital. She were too poorly for us to be allowed to visit her, an we didn't know when she'd be coming out again. If she was coming out again.

10. FRANCE

It were hard to imagine that a ship sinking so far away could change so much. But it did.

The Lusitania weren't no war ship. It was a passenger ship an the Germans had no right to go an sink it like they did. Over 1,000 folk died out there, lost in the cold, dark ocean. Just normal people. Women and children who ain't done nothing to no-one.

'Dirty beggers,' Birdy says, cleaning his gun for the third time as we was crossing to France on our own stinking ship. 'Just wait 'til I get out there. Them Huns ain't no better than rodents, ripe for poaching.'

'That could be our families,' says Jim, looking at me. 'Dying. It ain't right.'

Of course our family ain't never been on a big ship, or not even a small one to tell the truth. But I knowed what Jim were getting at. We all feeled the

75

same, thinking about our families an that. In part it was on account of the Lusitania, or course, but I knowed Jim was thinking about Mam being so sick. So was I. But I was thinking about me being sick an all. Trying not to throw up.

Three days it took us, nearly, to get to France. Three different trains just to get from Basingstoke down to Southampton, then onto the boat. A grey-painted Channel steamer that rolled an tossed all the way, with the smell of diesel an every body throwing up an that. Except Jim, of course. He said all railwaymen loved that smell. It was the smell of a good engine he reckoned. That made me feel worse, and as if things weren't bad enough, there was all that talk of the Lusitania. I was waiting for a German torpedo at every moment.

In France we had to march through the night 'til we reached camp. I reckon my face must've been grey as ash. My eyes was flickering and I couldn't help my head nodding forward then bobbing back up, again an again. My feet put themselves one in front of the other all by themselves, and my bad leg ached something terrible.

'How was your night?' Jim asked next morning, when we was looking for the canteen with Birdy. 'The ground here ain't as soft as them beds back in Basingstoke, is it?'

I pulled my cap a bit forward to keep the rain out of my eyes, an tried to smile. We'd spent the night in an old bell tent, except there weren't that much of the night left by the time we got there. Twelve men was squashed in that tent, laid out in a circle with our feet meeting in the middle. Even so, I reckon I felled asleep as soon as I hit the ground. But it didn't last. Most straight off I woked with a start, and lay there 'til sunrise just listening to a soft booming noise, like thunder a long way away. I knowed that were artillery. Big guns. I didn't know if it were ours or theirs, or both. But somewhere there was a battle going on and men like us was lying in trenches as them shells come pouring down.

'It weren't too bad,' I lied.

But I weren't really thinking about war by then, as we spotted the canteen.

'She will get well again. Won't she? Mam, I mean.'

'Course she will, Noggin,' Jim says. 'Take more than a cough to stop our mam.'

That made it a bit easier to smile. But then Jim stopped still, an I turned to face him. He were holding his ear. I knowed what that meaned. Listen.

'What?' I asked. 'What is it, Jim?'

Birdy pulled his tunic collars up and headed off.

'I ain't standing here in the pissing rain,' he says. 'I'll leave you two to have your little brotherly get together. I'm starving.'

Jim were looking down, an pursed his lips as Birdy trotted off. After a second, he speaked.

'Mam,' he says. 'It's Mam. There's something I gotta tell you.'

That made me feel sick, almost straight off. I feeled the colour going out of my face, an my mouth turning dry. He'd just said she were going to be alright. What else were there to tell? Real slow, his face lifted and he looked me in the eye. His huge shoulders was sagging.

'I'm sorry, Noggin,' he says. 'She didn't want you in the army. And I was to try to get you sent home.'

Different feelings rushed through me. Now I really didn't know what he was getting at, but it was like the nerviness was changing into something else. More quizzing going on in my head. I feeled my eyebrows frowning.

'What are you saying Jim?

'The shoes,' he says. 'Your shoes. That were my fault. And the report to the police. About you being underage an all.'

My mouth dropped open. I heared the words, but I were having a real hard time believing it. Jim didn't wait for me to say anything.

'It was what Mam wanted. Dad telled me in the letters. I didn't know what else to do.'

A picture of my shoes up there on the flagpole filled my head. My brother. My big brother had done that to me, not Adams, like I thought. And he'd lied about what Dad's letters was saying an all. I shut my eyes an pushed my cap up on my head, letting the rain dribble down my face, over my eyes, my lips. Jim didn't say nothing else. My belly was a horrid mixture of wanting to cry, an wanting to scream with anger at the same time. I waited a minute, then looked at him.

'So that was why your name was on that paper,' I says slowly, remembering what Sergeant Hodson had said outside the Captain's office. 'And why my letter was behind the curtains at home?'

He nodded, and carried on.

'And it were why I weren't talking to you all that time,' he added. 'Figured you'd get fed up and chuck it all in. Go home, like Mam wanted.'

Right then, I felt like I could chuck it in. Just turn around an walk away. It was too much in my head. Too many confusing thoughts all at once. But then I had a different thought.

'So,' I says, biting my lip an pointing at my big brother. 'So what made you stop, an start talking to me again? Being friendly like.'

Jim took in a deep breath.

'Dad,' he says. 'Dad wrote an told me about Mam having to stay in hospital on account of her sickness getting much worse. Said I was to look after you.'

I weren't expecting that. Mum was worse?

'What?' I says. 'When? When did he tell you that?'

Jim didn't say nothing for a moment or two. Then he speaked, real quiet.

'Few months back. About Christmas time.'

I gasped, like the air were squeezed out of my throat, an stared wide eyed. All that time. All that time he knowed about Mam being even more sick. And he lied to me about it. I turned away, pulling my cap off an rubbing my head with the rain.

'And Birdy,' I asked, without looking back at him. 'Suppose Birdy was acting cross with me back then 'cause of you an all?'

'No,' says Jim. 'That's just Birdy.'

*

Grey. It was all grey. From what I could see, France weren't no different than back in England, 'specially the weather. Rain an more rain, and dirt an mud everywhere, and army as far as you could see. Millions of them bell tents, all as cold and leaky as ours, I reckon. In fact, the whole Territorial Infantry Camp was grey an tatty. Nothing like the camp at Basingstoke, especially the canteen.

'It's disgusting,' was how Birdy seed it, back in our tent. 'Stinks of rotten food an sweat. And I can't eat that shit they're trying to tell us is food.'

By the time Sergeant Hodson comed in with a few Orderlies, I didn't care about any of it much anyway. My head were filled with what Jim said.

'Stand easy, lads,' says the Sergeant. 'Your time here is to be spent engaging in strict Assault Training, and I'm going to leave you in the capable hands of these gentlemen. Your instructors.'

I looked at the Orderlies. There was three of 'em, two quite young an one older, all wearing yellow armlets to show they was instructors.

'You useless little bleeders,' was the first words the older one shouts at us, after Sergeant Hodson had gone off.

The man cracked a leather-covered swagger stick against his leg.

'Attention!'

We all jumped to it, and did our best to stand to attention in the tent, an salute an that. But it weren't good enough. All three instructors shouted at us, mainly about how scruffy and stupid we was and about the tent being the worst mess they'd ever seen in all their life. Then they told us to strip.

At first we all just looked at each other. That made them blow their stack.

'NOW!' One of 'em bellows. 'Every filthy scrap. Off!'

I don't think I ever got to know the names of them

instructors. They might've told us, but mostly they was just there, one or other of 'em, face scrunched up an shouting. Always shouting.

It turned out everyone called 'em Canaries, on account of the yellow arm bands they weared. We took to calling the older bloke Cock Canary, an the others his Chicks. Mostly when we talked though, it didn't matter which one was which. Canary did this, Canary did that, was about all we ever said. Not to their faces, mind.

We done as we was told. I stood by my bed roll with the back of my head pressing up into the tent. I covered my privates with my hands, and felt a flushing over my face. Cock Canary snapped at the Chicks, telling them to start their examination. Then he strutted around looking everyone up an down.

'What in the name of all that's Holy are you?' He shouts at Birdy. 'I've seen more muscle on a chicken leg.'

'Sorry, staff,' says Birdy, stood right next to me, an not giving a monkey's about what he were showing.

'Sorry?' Says the instructor, sticking himself right in front of Birdy's face. 'You're sorry? What exactly have you got to be sorry for, boy? Eh?'

He were taller than me an Birdy, and thick set like an overgrown terrier. His moustache looked like it were waxed, and the yellow instructor's band round his arm was faded an grubby. I could smell that he'd had a proper breakfast that morning.

'And what are you looking at soldier?' He says, turning real fast to me.

My heart was in my mouth. I didn't know what to say. But at that moment, one of the other Chicks reached me, an the older one turned away, shouting an kicking things about the tent.

The Canary Chick checked my hair for lice, then my feet for any wrongs. That weren't all though.

'Turn around,' he says. 'And bend over.'

After a bit, everyone had been checked. All over. I stood there an stared straight ahead. Didn't want to look at any other body. Didn't want anyone looking at me. After more shouting, the Canaries strutted out again, leaving us with orders to sort everything before they comed back. I grabbed my pants, quick as I could.

'What do they expect,' Birdy says. 'We've only been here a few hours for God's sake.'

'I don't like 'em. Them Canaries,' says Sadsack. 'Who let 'em out of their cage?'

We all laughed at that, an got on with the tidying up. I sorted my space soon enough, but got in a flap trying to sort my webbing 'cause it had tangled up somehow.

'Here,' says Jim, grabbing at one of the webbing

straps 'That just needs to go through here.'

But I pulled away, yanking the strap out of his hand.

'Get off,' I said. 'I don't need no help from you.'

11. TOWNIES

We didn't have no dinner, nor no tea neither. That weren't on account of the canteen. It were 'cause of the Canaries. Every time they comed back to the tent, it weren't clean enough, or we wasn't smart enough. By the end of the day, they had us polishing the backs of all our buttons. And they checked every one of 'em an all. One spec of grime and we all had to start over an do it all again.

'I don't care what they says,' says Birdy when we was bunked down that night. 'I'm bloomin' starving. This rotten country must have rabbits mustn't it?'

I turned over, so I were looking at Birdy. He were sitting up an I could just see his sticking out ears against the pale canvas of the tent.

'What d'you mean, Birdy?' I whispered.

'I'll tell you what I mean,' he says back. 'I've got a gun haven't I. First thing tomorrow, I'm going out to bag us some bleedin' breakfast.'

'Go to sleep Birdy,' Jim's voice speaked out in the dark. 'You ain't got no bullets.'

That weren't going to stop Birdy. When we was waked by the bugle at reveille, which were real early, there weren't no sign of him nowhere.

He still hadn't showed when we was supposed to be heading off for morning roll call. And missing role call was a chargeable offence. Jim might've had an idea about what we could do. I thought about asking him. But I didn't.

Heading out to the Bull Ring, which is what they called the drill ground, I could feel the heat working its way up my leg. It were going to be a bad leg day. I knowed it.

There was hundreds of men all over. Probably thousands actually. We had to line up in a group with near on two hundred others. A whole Company, with our platoon and three other platoons an all. B Company, we was called. All the while, I was looking over my shoulder for Birdy, my hands clenching hard. But Sergeant Hodson was already there. Next to him, was our three Canaries.

'Come on Birdy,' I muttered to myself. 'Where are you?'

Then I seed him. He was rushing over, pulling his webbing on and with his gun as clean as ever. I feeled myself relax. I could've laughed. But I thinked too soon. Cock Canary spotted Birdy same moment I did. By the time Birdy joined the ranks next to me, the Canaries was all there waiting.

'Well,' Says Cock Canary. 'Parade a bit early for you, is it soldier?'

Birdy didn't say nothing. He was in trouble, an there weren't nothing he could do about it. If he speaked now, he'd get shouted at. If he didn't speak he'd still get shouted at. That was how it was. The Canaries ruled the camp. We all knowed it, even Sergeant Hodson. I took a breath and stared straight ahead, hoping I wouldn't be next.

'What, no answer? Lost for words are you lad?'

But the bellowing were gone, an the Canary's voice quieted right down. I blinked with surprise. Out the corner of my eye, I seed Birdy's shoulders soften an all. The instructor beckoned him forward and took him off through the ranks, an arm round his shoulder. His voice turned almost kind.

'That's a very clean gun, son. Where're you from?'

As they walked away from me, I heared Birdy.

'Wiltshire, Staff,' he says. 'I'm from Wiltshire.'

My heart sank, an I weren't alone. I reckon I could hear a groan from every other bloke in the Company. We was the Wiltshire Regiment. We was all from Wiltshire.

'Are you now? Well, fancy that.'

They carried on walking, 'til they was about fifty yards ahead of the rest of us. We was all looking at each other, wondering what was going on. Then Cock Canary turned an walked back, leaving Birdy standing out there facing us. All on his own.

The soft voice was gone.

'Right you little sods,' he shouts at us, an I can't help feeling he's looking at me. 'Any more of you snivelling bumpkins got anything smart to say?'

I stood still as I were able.

'Or can we get on with some bleedin' Assault Training?'

Nobody said a word, which maked the cheeks above Cock Canary's moustache turn bright red. He blowed through his nose like a steam shunter, sticked his chin an chest out, and bellowed from right down in his belly.

'WELL? Can we?'

I almost jumped.

'Yes Staff!' We all shouted back, loud as you like.

'Right,' he carries on, turning an pointing to Birdy. 'Now, you see our little genius over there. Since he clearly thinks I'm a bleedin' idiot, telling me he's from Wiltshire, I think we need to remind him which regiment he belongs to, don't you?'

Then he telled us what was to happen next. We

was to fix bayonets and charge towards Birdy shouting *Wiltshires* at the top of our voices. Birdy had to hold his gun up above his head, both arms straight up, an stand perfectly still. One of the Chicks standed behind him, to make sure he didn't slack none.

'And since you're all too green to know what it's like charging the Hun, he says. 'Just imagine you're chasing a fox off your farm with your pitchfork. Simple enough for you yokels?'

Somebody coughed. My heart leaped. It were Jim, an it was clear that he were going to say something, couldn't help himself. I shut my eyes, couldn't believe he could be so stupid. Then I snapped 'em open again, and looked to the Canaries. Maybe they hadn't heard.

They had. Slowly, the other Chick's stare moved round 'til it landed on Jim's face, sticking up there above all them around him.

'Well, now. What have we got here?' The Canary says, pushing through to where Jim was. 'That a bit much for you, my oversized cowpoke?'

'No, Staff,' says Jim, staring straight ahead. 'I mean... It's just that..'

'Yes? Something to say?'

'It's just that some of us ain't farmers, Staff,' Jim pushed on, even though he must've known he were for it now. 'From the railways. Apprentice engineer. We live in the town.'

I could feel my leg aching, an just waited for the explosion to come. But Cock Canary had other ideas, and walked forward to join the Chick in front of Jim. The two of 'em chatted for a second, then asked for everyone from Town to come forward. There was about forty of us, I reckon, and we was all to come out of the ranks and sit on the ground behind Birdy, in the misty rain. Jim first.

'Well excuse me,' is what Cock Canary said. 'Can't expect our posh Townies to lower themselves with common old Assault Training, can we? You sit down over there and take it easy. You can thank Private Engineer here for bringing your lofty status to my attention.'

The ground were muddy and, soon enough, the damp comed through my greatcoat an tunic an trousers. But we weren't to move. William Adams was there an all, of course, with a couple of lads who was clearly his cronies. He stared at Birdy as we was walking by, but he never speaked, not until we was all sitting an the Canaries had gone back to the rest of the Company.

'This ain't good,' he mutters through gritted teeth. 'We's for the high jump, James Arkell, thanks to you. You see if we ain't.'

Jim didn't say nothing back. I knowed Adams was right, though.

We all just sat there and watched as the Company charged at poor Birdy. Then they had to stand to attention, about turn and quick march back to where they started. It weren't long before Birdy's skinny arms took to shaking, holding up that precious gun of his. Every time he lowered it, the rest of the Company had to charge again. And again. And again. By the end, Birdy were almost screaming. I could feel tears stinging behind my eyes. The Canaries didn't pay no heed though, just kept 'em at it.

It was late into the day before they marched the main body off, and let Birdy go an all. But the rest of us was to stay where we was, soaked to the skin an cold right through. By the time the Canaries comed back, it were almost dark.

'Now then, my highfalutin engineers,' Cock Canary says, and I swear there were a smile under that waxy moustache. 'I've arranged a special fatigue for you. One suited to your particular skills. On your feet. Snap to it.'

*

We all knowed about coal, or course. Even them few who didn't really have no connection to the works was used to seeing the great black piles of it. If you lived in Town, you couldn't miss 'em. We was still surprised to see the stacks in the camp, though. Of course, they weren't nothing like the ones we was used to, but they was still a fair size.

'Tractors,' says one of the men, pointing.

We all looked. I squinted in the dark and could make out the black shapes of rows of traction engines alongside the coal stacks. Steam driven, of course. Which meaned they needed coal. I heared Jim's voice.

'Coal to feed their fires,' he says. 'Heat up the boilers, and make the steam that turns the wheels.'

I slowly shaked my head. My brother who spent so much time saying nothing at all. Didn't he know when to shut up?

'Silence in the ranks,' snaps a Canary. 'Not that it's any of your concern, but they're for pulling artillery pieces. They're back here for repair.'

As we walked along, the huge tractors looked down on us against the night sky, one after the other. The smell of oil and grease filled my nose, an I thinked of them dark works. If these was just ones that was broken, how many was out there dragging guns to shell the Hun? And did the Hun have as many for shooting at us? My stomach felt sick.

'Now,' says Cock Canary, stopping us in front of a coal stack about twenty feet across an ten feet high. 'I'm glad you all know about coal. Makes this very easy. Basically, I want this pile moved, to over there.'

He pointed to an empty space, right next to where the stack was already.

The Chicks marched us to a shed where we had to get shovels. Of course, they managed to find an extra large one for Jim. Cock Canary pushed his sleeve up an twisted his arm, to see his watch.

'You've got about seven hours before tomorrow's reveille,' he barked. 'Get on with it.'

We all just standed there, as the three of 'em walked off. I looked at the stack. My body was aching so bad, but I could feel my belly puffing in an out, faster than it should, and my teeth grating against each other. Jim was just standing there. At that moment, I hated the sight of him. Then Adams walked up to him, his mates behind him, just like it always was back in Town.

'I'm going to do my share,' Adams hissed, pressing his shovel against Jim's chest and staring up into his face. 'But I ain't going to forget this, Arkell. Mark my words.'

12. FOOTBALL

We never proper recovered after that coal moving fatigue. All through the night I were thinking we'd get to go to sleep when we was done. But that weren't how things worked at the Territorial Infantry Camp. Not with them Canaries. We never got clean neither. That coal dust left us with grey faces an grey hands for ages. And the Canaries wouldn't give us leave to shower, instead they took to calling us Sooty Platoon.

'It's 'cause them Canaries ain't gonna actually fight the Hun themselves,' one of our lads reckoned. 'And we is. That bothers 'em, so they takes it out on us.'

That was what everyone else reckoned an all. Yellow was the right colour for 'em.

One good thing though, were that Birdy had actually managed to catch some game, even without bullets. When we got back to the tent with that black grit all over, our mess tins was on our bed rolls with pieces of boiled duck in 'em. Nothing ever tasted so good.

Mind you, that were about the only bit of decent food we ever got in that place. Rest of the time, my tummy were rumbling non-stop.

After a couple of weeks, we was dead on our feet. I couldn't hardly tell when I was having bad leg days. Both legs ached all the time, an every other bit of me an all. Just going from one thing to the next, an not just marching and drill an that, like back on the Plain or at Basingstoke. Things was more to do with the war proper. Fighting skills, especially hand-to-hand, which meaned boots an teeth and elbows an anything else you could muster. It usually meaned blood an bruises an all. And broken bones for some. Then there was rolling out barbed wire, and rolling it back up again, an trench storming. Even though we didn't have no trenches there, on account of the ground being too sandy. That didn't stop the Canaries from making us charge a red tape line laid out across the ground. It didn't stop 'em making us dig neither. Some days we spent the whole time digging in the sand, just for it to pour back down into the hole again. The Canaries always made sure Jim had the biggest shovel, an told him to dig harder. Serves him right.

Only once did we get rest time. The strange thing

was that none of us wanted to use the time for extra shuteye. It was like that time were so precious, we wanted to make the most of it.

'Footie!' Some of the lads shouted.

Even though I didn't have no interest in playing, I went along with it, choosing to watch. I figured if they tried to force me to play, then they'd just have to put up with me being rubbish. But, as it happened, no-one did, and me and Sadsack and a load of others sat on the sidelines.

Teams was divided by Platoon or Company, and in the end, the whole Bull Ring turned into one giant football pitch. A hundred men or more on each side including some officers, and Canaries acting like referees. All charging, shouting an kicking. Half was wearing shirts. The others, skins. With the sand being stirred up, and the blur of men, it were near impossible to tell who were winning or losing. The only way I could follow the ball was from the crowding round it, an the noise.

'Out the way you beggers,' Sergeant Hodson shouted as the teams came charging towards where I were sitting.

I didn't have to be telled again. I knowed they wouldn't stop and we'd be trampled for sure. I jumped up an backed away, all the while cheering our team, the skins. As they poured towards me, I were able to spot Jim, towering above the rest and barging all an sundry out of his way as he closed in on the ball. His face still looked coal-dust grey, especially against the white of his bare chest, but his eyes was wild and he were shouting at the top of his voice, same as all them others. It were odd to see my brother playing like that. The only time I ever knowed him to have that look was when he was in one of his crazy moods. But I clearly seed half a smile there. He was enjoying every minute of it. I pulled back a bit behind Sadsack's shoulder. Jim didn't see me.

I was about to cheer our team again, when I spotted another grey faced skin out of the corner of my eye, coming in fast. Adams. His wiry figure weaved through the others, right behind Jim. For a moment I weren't sure what was going on, but there was that glint in Adams's green eyes, an I knowed he were up to no good. Revenge for the coal fatigue. Of course I still weren't happy with my brother about that, but I couldn't help wanting to shout out. Warn him. But before I were able, Adams' boot crashed down onto the back of Jim's heel. My brother crumbled, vanishing in a cloud of sand and boots an puttees an shouting.

In a moment the crowd was gone, with Adams in total control of the ball. I went towards where Jim was laid out. Birdy was there beside him, shouting out, telling that there'd been a foul. But I knowed the Canaries weren't bothered. That was just the sort of game it was. As it happened, there weren't no need to worry anyhow. Jim was up in a second rubbing his ankle, and him an Birdy trotted off towards the crowd.

As they got nearer the two piles of jackets that made up the shirts' goal line, another commotion started up. It seemed that someone had given Adams a taste of his own medicine. He were standing there holding the ball and shouting an pointing at the other players, demanding a penalty and starting to walk off down the pitch.

Only he didn't spot Birdy. In a blur, Birdy flew straight at him, his skinny arms flaying like a flywheel. Adams didn't know what was happening an tumbled to the ground. Birdy didn't stop. He crashed down, landing his knees on Adams' chest, both fists pounding an beating.

It were only a big hand on Birdy's shoulder that put an end to it.

'That'll do, Birdy,' Jim says, as he pulls him away. 'I think that's him well and truly sorted.'

But of course, it weren't quite that simple with Adams. He jumped up, clutching a bloody nose and shouting.

'He's boken by dose, de begger,' he squeals, looking to the Canaries. 'Ain't you gonna do anyfing?'

The Canaries weren't interested, mind. Cock Canary made it plain they weren't there to fight other people's battles for 'em. Just wanted the game to get on. Adam's weren't giving in that easy. He grabbed the ball up so the game couldn't carry on, and turned to his cronies.

'Well go on,' he says to them, pointing at Birdy and Jim. 'Get 'em den.'

A slight move from Jim, an a little twitch of his head, was more than enough to make Adams' so called friends decide it weren't worth the bother.

'We ain't got all day, you know' shouted one of the Canaries. 'Somebody get that ball, for God's sake.'

Everyone looked at Jim. Jim turned and looked at Birdy, and they gived each other a little nod.

Then, before Adams knowed what was happening, Jim was on him and had him scooped up in a bear hug, lifting him clear off the ground. Birdy grabbed his feet, an clutched them tight to stop 'em kicking out.

Without missing a stride, and ignoring Adams' high pitched squeals, the two of 'em marched straight to the shirts' goal mouth. The goalie leaped out the way, and Jim an Birdy tossed Adams over the line like a sack of coal into a bunker. Ball an all.

For a tiny moment there was silence. Then everyone went mad. The skins cheered, saying it were a goal, and the shirts shouted at the refs.

Of course it weren't a goal. But it didn't matter none, the game got on and the skins thrashed the shirts anyhow. As everyone headed back to their tents after, most of the gassing were about Birdy an my brother. Even Adams' cronies was talking of it. Especially on account of Jim's size and strength.

'The Huns are in for a shock when they meet that big'un,' I heared a bloke behind me saying. 'Glad he's on our side.'

I turned round.

'He's my brother,' I says, then dipped into the tent feeling a flush over my face.

The others was already there, cheering for Jim an Birdy, an their victory. The only shame was that there weren't no decent food for prizes, which meaned the winners got paid by the losers in barrels of ale. Course, most of the lads liked that, and they was happy to share it with the rest of us what didn't play.

'Come on Noggin,' Birdy says. 'Time to be a man. Get it down you.'

I tried it. But then spat it out, pulling a sour face.

'It's horrible,' I says. 'Real bitter!'

'That's the point,' Birdy laughed, along with the others. 'Real bitter!'

Then he pours me some more, an I tried again. It didn't get any nicer, but I kept on sipping at it, not wanting to be left out. It weren't long before Sadsack was strutting around the tent pretending he was Cock Canary.

'You little bleeders,' he shouted. 'You're all on a charge.'

Everyone laughed. I squatted on my bed roll and my eye caught Jim's. He smiled at me, an I smiled back. Couldn't help myself.

After that, the talking got harder to listen to, and I lay back, my head spinning an my guts feeling like they was going to chuck up any moment. Horrible pictures spinned round behind my eyes, and I cursed myself for drinking the beer. But I was glad me an Jim could smile at each other again, even if I hadn't full forgiven him for keeping secret about Mam. And I were glad when everyone else decided it were time to hit the sack, and the noises faded.

'I'm sorry lads,' I heared Birdy say. 'I would go poaching. But I think I may be too pissed.'

One or two grunted, but there weren't nothing else to be said, an I turned over and pulled my damp greatcoat over me. Just as I drifted off though, there was a noise. At first I didn't know what was going on, and rolled over too quick, tangling myself up.

A light was shining right in my face. As I tried to

block it out, I seed the shape of one of the Canaries standing there. He was shouting at me to get up.

'Up, you lazy bleeder,' he bellows, kicking me. 'Up!'

Of course, I had no choice but to do as he telled me and I soon seed the other Canaries was there, waking everyone else up. I was thinking it were just them being their usual horrible selves, and even had a few swear words going round my head. But when we got out to the Bull Ring I seed it weren't just us. It looked like everyone on the camp was coming out. Mass night manoeuvres. I feeled sick burbling up in my belly.

14. THE MAJOR'S MOTORCYCLE

Two hours we ran up them sandbanks, in full kit and with bayonets fixed. Then a rest, which we needed bad. Even though my eyes was used to the dark, it were impossible to see the end of the line of men we was sitting there with. It weren't just our Company, but maybe the whole Battalion we reckoned. I weren't too sure how many that was. Thousands though.

'Uh oh,' says Birdy, still tipsy, and taking a fag from the bloke next to him. 'Officers coming.'

I never seed Birdy smoke before, and he looked real funny puffing away on that badly rolled ciggy. It weren't no surprise, mind. Loads of them others smoked. It was like a hobby, something to do. It didn't appeal to me though. Don't reckon it would go down too well with Jim neither, if I was to start up. I turned to see what Birdy was talking about, and he were right. Our Canaries was marching along with a small crowd of others. When they comed near, I seed that our Company Commanders was there an all. Captain Roberts an Major Cromwell. We all clambered to our feet an stood to attention as they passed by us, smokers stubbing out their ciggies.

'So we have our very own engineers, do we?' I heared the Major say. 'From the railways, you say.'

'Yes sir,' snapped back Cock Canary. 'A few dozen of them, I'd say sir.'

'Jolly good. Send one over first thing tomorrow. I have a rather messy job that needs doing. There's a good man.'

It were obvious the minute he said it were a messy job who the Canaries would pick. Next morning, one of the Chicks comed in to get us on parade, and shouted out for Private Arkell.

'Special fatigue,' he says. 'Straight to the motor pool.'

Jim jumped to it. But before he reached the Canary, Sadsack shouted out.

'Which one?' He says. 'There's two Private Arkells, Staff.'

'Rats,' says the Chick. 'So there is.'

He took off his cap an scratched his head. Jim and me looked at each other. We both knowed Cock Canary meaned him to do it. At least I reckon he did.

'Right,' the Canary says. 'Both of you. On the

double. When they tell you which one is needed, make sure the other of you gets straight back to the Bull Ring. Go on, hop it!'

*

It took us best part of an hour to get to the motor pool, an even longer to find where we was supposed to be. We went past the rows of broken tractions engines and the coal piles, but neither of us said a word. Soon, we was amongst rows of motor lorries, muddled in with old carts and gun carriages and all manner of piles of crates, an engines and bits of machines an all. Everything stinked of oil and the sand was almost black under our boots.

We spotted an officer, a Scottish Lieutenant, in his kilt an all, and decided we should ask if he knowed where we should report.

'Sir, reporting for a job for Major Cromwell,' says Jim, saluting the Lieutenant, eyes straight ahead 'Private Arkell. That is, er, we're both Private Arkell.'

'Aye,' said the officer. 'I can see that. At ease.'

Jim stood at ease, with his hands smartly behind his back. But I didn't. My mouth were dropped open, an I was staring. If I did that with an officer on any normal day, I'd be on a charge, quick as you like. But the Lieutenant just pushed his round glasses up on his nose, an smiled.

'What,' I stutters. 'Edward. Edward Macpherson.

What are you doing here?'

Edward Macpherson. The same Edward Macpherson who had camped down in our front room. Now look at him, smart as you like. He laughed, and Jim suddenly realised who it was an all and we all shaked hands, even though we shouldn't really be talking to an officer that way.

'More to the point, Private Noggin,' Edward says. 'What are *you* doing here? How old are you, exactly? And weren't you planning to get yourself off to be educated?'

I shifted from one leg to the other, putting my hands in my pockets then taking 'em out again. Jim was grinning and took off his hat and rubbed his head.

'Yes, I mean, no,' I says, choosing to ignore the middle question. 'I, er, I joined the army.'

'Yes,' says Edward, smiling. 'I worked that out all for myself. So now you're both engineers, here to fix Cromwell's machine are you?'

We both nodded.

'Good, good. I think he's in the workshop right now. Come on, follow me.'

We more or less trotted after Edward Macpherson. I stared at his smart uniform, with its tartan. Couldn't believe someone I knowed, who'd lived in our house, were an officer. He strolled off at quite a rate to where there was a load of long wooden sheds, with corrugated iron roofs. Inside was full of stuff going on, with vehicles all over an soldiers, Royal Engineers, all fixing, carrying or working on something. Just like the works at home. Jim gasped as he gawped around at everything.

Down the end, Edward showed us into another, smaller area, walled off from the main hall. Major Cromwell was there, talking to two other men. He ignored us for a minute, then turned and spoke to Edward, frowning over a pair of little glasses what sat on the end of his nose with a cord hanging off 'em.

'Yes, Lieutenant,' he snapped. 'What is it?'

Edward stood to attention an saluted. Me an Jim did the same.

'Sir,' he says. 'These men have been sent for a special job for you, sir.'

That made the Major's face change. The glasses fell off his nose an he turned to us with a smile, now ignoring the two blokes he were talking to.

'Ah, splendid!' he says, in the poshest voice I ever heared. 'I've been waiting for you. This way gentlemen. This way. Thank you Macpherson.'

Me an Jim never been called gentlemen before. Well, I hadn't. Jim may've been. Edward winked at me, as me an Jim followed the Major. He took us to a motorcycle, leaning against the wall. I'd not seen a motorcycle up that close before, but I knowed this one weren't in good shape.

'Bit of a prang, I'm afraid,' he says to us, stroking his chin and staring at the machine. 'But can't get a flaming Royal Engineer around here, not for all the tea in China. Plain daft, if you ask me. Surrounded by the wretched creatures, but all too bally busy. Ruddy war. Damn nuisance.'

The bike was a Douglas, the Major's own personal machine. Jim squatted down next to it, already pushing his sleeves up and his eyes looking like they was going to pop out of his head.

'Twin cylinders. In cast iron,' he says, maybe thinking I was interested. 'Three hundred and forty eight c.c., and three-speed gearbox an all.'

'Quite right, young man,' says the Major, clapping Jim on the shoulder. 'She's my pride and joy. You clearly know your bikes, so I'll leave you chaps to it. See what you can do for her, will you.'

Jim jumped up again, an we both saluted as the officer went off.

'He's slammed it into something, silly begger,' says Jim as soon as we was alone. 'But reckon we can sort it. Come on, Noggin. Time for you to be an apprentice mechanic.'

He smiled with that. I didn't though. But Jim were too caught up with the bike to notice, already pulling it away from the wall to have a look at the other side.

'The front forks have been shoved right back,' he says, tapping at something with his finger. 'And the wheel's bent that thing right over.'

He were right, of course. Even I could see that much. Not only was the front wheel pushed right back to one side, next to the engine, everything else at the front was twisted an all. Handlebars, levers, cables, all skewed. An the brass headlamp, with a little peak what should've been sticking out, was all squashed up. Whether there were more damage, mechanical an that, I wouldn't know. Just had to hope Jim would. Though it were hard to understand just how his training for the railways would make him an expert in motorcycles. Far as I knowed, he'd never been any closer to one than I had.

In the end, he set to the bike with a load of spanners what he borrowed from the Royal Engineers in the main shed, and gave me the headlamp to try to straighten out with a little hammer and pair of pliers. In truth, I sort of enjoyed it. Just sitting there in a warm, dry building was nice enough. Especially knowing our mates would all be out in the Bull Ring with the Canaries shouting at 'em an making them charge up and down all day.

'That's not bad,' Jim says, looking at my handiwork. 'Course it ain't perfect, but reckon the

Major will be happy enough. I think I've done too. Just need your help to straighten out the forks.'

Jim made me sit on the bike, an he sat on the floor in front of it with his legs stretched out either side.

'Push your feet down hard, Noggin,' he says, gripping the forks with his huge hands. 'And keep that brake pulled right in. Don't want the bike to move any.'

Then he tugged. I was half thinking it would take a moment or two to get going. But I didn't allow for Jim putting his whole strength in straight off. His body yanked back, and the bike lurched forward between his legs, dragging my boots across the concrete floor. I was still gripping the brake lever, and peered over the handlebars. Jim was lying practically flat, and the front wheel was just about as far up between his legs as it could've been. Jim lifted his head and looked down.

'Phew,' he says. 'That were a bit close for comfort.'

He looked up at me, and we both grinned.

But the forks was still bent.

'Let's turn it over,' Jim suggested, after a few other attempts. 'We should get a better grip if the whole thing's upside down. And we can take the front wheel off too, to get at the forks properly.'

It seemed like a good idea, after we'd taken the petrol tank off and let all the oil out of the engine.

Only when Jim pulled on the forks, they still wouldn't straighten out, an as he tugged, the whole bike still inched along the floor. Even with me trying to hold it back. Soon, we had to give it up. There were a chance it might start to scrape the leather of the saddle, and maybe even bend the upside down handlebars.

We heared the click of heels on the hard floor and turned to see Lieutenant Edward Macpherson coming.

'Coffee, chaps?' He says, as he reached us, holding two steaming mugs. 'How's it going? All okay I trust?'

Jim explained and Edward wished us luck and left us to get on with it, saying he were sure we'd sort it.

Me an Jim just sat there, drinking our coffee. Hot, real coffee. Served by an officer. We'd never known anything like it. It were real bitter an made me purse my lips, but I loved every sip.

'I've got an idea,' I says, after a bit.

Jim looked at me, an raised his eyebrows, quizzing me like. But I just stared back at him, chewing my lip and feeling the warmth of the coffee mug. Then I sort of nodded, plonked down the cup an got up.

'Back in a minute,' I says.

Then I was gone, before Jim had a chance to say anything. I didn't go far. Just out into the yard. In a minute I was back, holding a length of steel pipe almost as long as me, meaned for a traction engine chimney. Jim was standing there, waiting with a frown on his face. I ignored him and walked straight to the bike, struggling to raise the pipe up so I could lower its end down over the forks. Jim's face changed instantly, eyes wide and mouth open in surprise, as he twigged what I were up to.

'Leverage,' he says, giving me a hand. 'Noggin, that's brilliant.'

And it worked an all. The extra length given by the pipe meaned all we had to do was pull on its top and the forks slowly unbent, like they weren't made of metal at all. All the while, I gabbled away like a steam tappet. By the time we'd turned her back up, put the tank back on, and cleaned an polished every inch, I were almost bubbling with pride inside. Last, we clipped on the shiny brass lamp. Jim clapped me on the back.

'Excellent job, little brother. Dad would be proud of you,' he says.

Then he sent me to find the Major, to tell him we was done, while he taked the tools back to the Royal Engineers. I looked all over, but there weren't no sign of the Major, only Edward Macpherson. He were standing by the hall entrance, talking to another soldier. Even though the other man had his back to me, I spotted that yellow armband straight off, and knowed who it were.

As Cock Canary turned an seed me, his cap peak raised up with his eyebrows an his moustache twitched. He weren't happy.

15. BAYONET PRACTICE

A couple of weeks we reckoned, before we was going to be moving out. The whole Battalion, maybe six thousand of us. Of course, our first thoughts should've been about the Hun. We all knowed where we would be going. To the Front. To the war proper. Not that they telled us anything, it were just that we seed other areas of the camp emptying real quick, men packing up and heading off in Full Battle Order. We knowed it would come round to us soon. We was soldiers after all, an the whole reason we was there was to fight the Germans. Stop them in their push into France.

Thoughts of danger, and even death, did sneak into my head, especially at night. But the biggest feeling was excitement. Some of that were 'cause we was going to do what we was trained to do, after all that time. Most of all, though, it were excitement at getting away from the Territorial Infantry Camp. From the Bull Ring. From the Canaries. We couldn't wait.

'Anyone got any spare gun oil?' Says Birdy. 'Mine's run out already. Useless.'

Everyone laughed. Only Birdy could've cleaned his gun so much that he'd run out of oil. The rest of us had hardly started our supply of the stuff. I turned to offer him some of mine, but Jim was already there, pouring some into Birdy's can from his own. The two of 'em was talking, wide eyed, like all of us. Excited. But then Jim's face changed, losing all the colour. Even accounting for them coal stains, he looked greyer still. He was staring at Birdy, but not listening anymore. He turns and comed towards me, bringing the oil can with him.

I stopped cleaning my own Smelly, an asked him what was up.

'Oil,' he says, looking at his can. 'I didn't put no oil back in the bike.'

I weren't sure exactly what that meant, but it were clear bothering him.

'A motorbike with no oil...'

He looked at me, but his eyes weren't on me at all. I heared his breathing, real deep.

'That'll be alright, won't it?' I says back to him, trying to catch his focus. 'Sure the Major looks after that sort of thing. He must be used to it, mustn't he?'

Jim looked at me for a moment, then let out a breath an his shoulders relaxed a bit.

'You're right, Noggin,' he says, his eyes looking at me proper almost. 'It's a total loss system. Oil drains through the engine all the while it's going. He must fill it up before every trip. Has to.'

Only it turned out he hadn't.

'Arkell,' screams Cock Canary, when we's all lined up for bayonet practice in the Bull Ring. 'Get out here, NOW!'

Me an Jim looked at each other, and both started through the ranks. Jim tried waving me back. He clear thinked it were him the instructor wanted. But Cock Canary weren't thinking that way.

'Not you, Arkell,' he shouts at Jim. 'Back in line. It's your little begger of a brother I want.'

It was a bad leg day. I did what I could not to limp, as I walked out and stood in front of the three Canaries. Cock Canary's face was red, and I swear I could smell the anger off his breath as he bellowed right in my face.

'Fix bayonet!' He shouts at me.

I fumbled with the Smelly, and tries to get my bayonet out as quick as I could. But it weren't quick enough, and the Chicks shouted at me an all, which made it even harder. I did get it on, after another try, and pulled myself up smartish to attention.

Cock Canary cursed under his breath at me, then shouts again, pointing behind him at the wooden frames what was holding up our practice targets.

'Them things hanging over there,' he shouts. 'May look like sacks of straw to you, you ignorant git. But they ain't, do you hear. They is the Devil himself. The Hun. And your job is to have his innards out with that 1907 Pattern bayonet that we so kindly let you have.'

Then he poked his stick in my chest.

'And now, Private Engineer Ruddy Arkell, you can show us all how it's done.'

My heart pounded in my chest. I wanted to look behind me, like he were talking about some other soldier. But I knowed it were only me.

'And there's one very special Hun up there, just for you. Off you go.'

Through that moustache, something like a grin appeared. I looked past him. It was then that I seed one of the frames didn't have a sack hanging from it. There was something else, smaller an round. The rest of the lads must've only noticed it at the same moment, 'cause there was a gasp from 'em all. It was their football.

I stared at the Canary for a moment, then my eyes flicked to where Sergeant Hodson was. But his body sagged an he looked at me and pursed his lips. There weren't nothing he could do. The Canaries ruled the camp. My guts knotted up and everything went blurry like. I could feel that hot feeling working its way up my leg.

'What you waiting for?' Cock Canary says. 'A flaming invitation? You never done bayonet practice before?'

'No Staff,' I says, shaking my head. 'I can't. I mean yes Staff. But please Staff.'

I seed his mouth opening, and I knowed I were going to be in more trouble. Instead of him speaking, though, he lifted his swagger stick and cracked it down across the back of my neck. The sting of that leather-covering made a tear come to my eye. I put my head down, holded my gun like we'd been trained, and ran. My leg was stiff, but it weren't as bad as it could've been, an I just kept going, straight at the football. The Chicks ran alongside me, shouting all the while. I felt sick.

The bayonet found its mark, and I shoved it hard into the tanned leather, feeling it burst under the sharpened blade. My teeth was gritted, an all I could think of was all them others standing behind me. Watching and hating me. But that weren't enough for the Canaries. I had to swing my arms back then forward again an again, sometimes missing the thing altogether, sometimes ripping its guts open even worse.

After, I turned and marches back, all the while trying not to look up. I didn't want to see them faces watching. But Cock Canary weren't done with me yet. He was whacking his leg with his stick.

'What on God's Earth was that supposed to be, soldier?' He says. 'And what sort of running do you call that?'

'Sorry, Staff?' I spluttered out, trying to stand to attention proper like.

He pushed his face right in front of mine.

'You think you can skive off and mess around with an officer's vehicle, do you?' He spits. 'And then fail to follow the most basic mechanics. Like oil!'

He poked me in the chest with his stick. Of course, he were there when I told Lieutenant Macpherson the bike was done. He thinked it was me what forgot about the oil. Didn't know Jim was there an all.

'You left your commanding officer stranded, soldier. With a broken down bike just a few miles from the enemy lines! How do you think that looks for us, eh?'

I tried to look to Jim, but Cock Canary poked me again, an almost pushed me off my feet

'So don't give me your pathetic apologies you little bag of piss,' he says.

He then turned away from me and marches off a way. At first I thinks maybe he were going to check what I done to the football. But he stopped short, an turned back to face me.

'Again, Private,' he shouts. 'This time, let's see how you cope with a real target.'

He slapped his belly with his stick, and I knowed what he wanted me to do. My mouth were dry, but I knowed I didn't have no choice.

'Refusing an order, soldier?' He bellows at me.

'No, Staff,' I shouts back, pulling myself upright as I were able and facing my eyes straight ahead.

'Well? What the heck are you waiting for?

I grinded my teeth together.

'Please leg,' I mutters to myself, lifting my foot up and down a bit. 'Please do as I needs you to.'

Then I stamped it hard as I could against the earth. The shock ran all up to my hip, and before I had time to wince from the pain, I throwed myself forward, running best I could and trying to get a proper shout out. In front of me, Cock Canary just stood there, waiting.

Then I feels everything going fuzzy and a red swelling up in my guts. My shouting turned to yelling, screaming. Screaming so it hurt my mouth to make the noise, and with my eyelids feeling like they's ripping wide open. I forgot all about my leg and ran like I never ran before.

I reached Cock Canary in no time, and swinged that gun forward, aiming that bayonet right at his black heart. My arms was tensed so hard it almost felt like they was going to tear off in that second when I striked. I pushed forward off my toes with my whole body, each bit of me wanting to see that steel blade tear into the Canary's guts and rip him open.

But there wasn't no gut ripping. No blood. Cock Canary just steps aside and I rushed past him and stumbled forward. As I did, I felt the full weight of that stick again. Across the side of my face. I lost control and stabbed the bayonet into the ground, right up to its hilt. My chest smacked into the butt of the gun and knocked the breath right out of me.

I pulled myself up, clutching my face an chest, and turned around.

'Five days Confined to Barracks,' Cock Canary says, before turning back to the others. 'For hesitating to obey an order.'

16. ON A CHARGE

I was used to being tired out, and to carrying on anyway. After my big accident on the railway sleeper it were two years before I got to walk again, without crutches. Even so, I weren't allowed to just sit about all that time.

The doctors didn't know what to do with me. There weren't any use me being in hospital no more, they said. Something wrong with my spine what affected the nerves down my legs, one leg worse than the other. That were all they could say. All they could do. But Mam weren't going to leave it at that.

First she had Dad and Uncle Phil make a special bed for me, out of two lengths of sleeper they got from the works. Them sleepers was laid down side by side with a gap in the middle. It meaned I could lay flat on my back, without damaging my spine no more. It was Mam's idea. Though she didn't like the idea of using sleepers. Nor did I.

'Hair of the dog,' Dad called it. 'Sleepers made the problem. Now sleepers can help make it better again.'

I lay on that hard bed for a year or more. Mam had to help me with everything. Including all the private stuff, which I hated. But she weren't going to let me get lazy. All the time, she was reading stuff to me, and asking me questions. And every day she made me do exercises. Even though them doctors thinked there weren't no hope. They was wrong. At the end of that first year, Dad fetched a pair of crutches from the works, where they was made in the wood shop for injured workers. Mam made me use 'em all the time, even when I was real tired. Bit by bit, my legs got better and stronger an stronger. They might never get healed altogether, but I reckon all the army training were much the same, helping 'em get stronger still. Though of course that didn't mean I didn't have bad leg days, when that hot feeling worked its way up my leg. When I was tired out proper. And five days Confined to Barracks was about as tiring as it got.

Only I don't know why they call it that. We didn't have no barracks proper, and I bare spent a minute inside anyway.

Every day I had to get up an hour before every other soldier and report to the Canaries in my full kit, with everything in its proper place, and my gun cleaned and oiled an all. Then I had to do the duties what they told me to do, which included running messages and cleaning kit for them and helping officers with any jobs they needed doing an all.

Half the day the Canaries had me doing their job of shouting *left right, left right* at drill. I had to do the drill an all, with every Company. It weren't so bad when it was others what was drilling. But it were my Company, that was the worst. The Canaries pushed them even harder than normal, and not one of 'em would even look at me. Every face looked like they thinked they was getting treated harsh 'cause of me. Especially now they'd lost their precious football an all.

I didn't get no chance to speak to Jim. When I did see him, his face was blank. Into one of his silent moods, an I just knowed he hadn't told anyone the whole truth about the Major's bike. That it weren't really my fault.

Every hour I had to run off to find one of the Canaries and report again. Didn't matter which one. They checked my kit and made sure I were dressed proper. If they found anything wrong it would be another punishment duty. I lost count of how many times I had to clean their latrines.

I didn't finish 'til after ten o'clock at night, when all the others was already tucked up an asleep. I collapsed onto my bed roll still wearing half my kit and not bothering to eat nothing neither.

On the first night or two, Sadsack sneaked over and tried to yank my boots off.

'Get off,' I says. 'Just leave 'em on.'

'Suit yourself,' he says and went back to his bunk.

But by the fourth night, I were so tired I didn't even notice and when I woked up, my boots was off and I had a blanket over me. At first I was thinking I were back at home, and had a bed of my own. I pulled the blanket round my neck and rolled over. I don't know how long I lay there for, but I woked up with a start when I realised I wasn't at home at all.

I looked around me, and scratched my head. My kit were all laid out, nice an neat like, with my uniform and webbing and kit all looking brand new, and my boots so shiny you'd think they was made of black glass. My gun was laid there an all, polished and greased up the way only Birdy could make a gun look. I reckon him and Sadsack must've been up half the night.

As I got my kit on, I looked around. Every other lad was sleeping. None of them moved. Then, inside one of my boots I finds something. I pulled it out. It were a fat bar of chocolate like I'd never had to myself before, ever. And there were a card. It weren't in an envelope so I knowed it must've come with a letter. It was in Dad's squiggly writing, an Jim must've opened it. But Mam had wrote in the card an all. It said, all neat like, *with all our love.*

I heared Birdy's voice whisper in the morning darkness.

'Happy birthday, Noggin,' he said.

That made me stop what I were doing, and I dropped back on the bed roll and just laid there holding that card against my chest, even though I didn't have time.

I didn't know that were what the date was. Birdy must've knowed it from seeing the card with Jim, and maybe guessed what had happened with the bike oil an that. Knowing Jim like he did. I huddled in a little ball and stared at the card with a lit match. It was full of kisses. Mam must be all right. A tear crawled down my cheek. I looked at the huge shape of Jim across the tent, lying there under his blanket, still an silent.

I wiped the back of my hand across my face, pulled myself together and went off to report to the Canaries. But they wasn't there, an I had to report to Sergeant Hodson instead. He told me I was about the smartest soldier he'd seen all week. That made it feel proper like a birthday.

*

There was still one thing we had to do before we was ready for heading to the Front. Live shooting. It meaned being trained by other canaries, and they was real different to ours. Course, the rifle instructors was even stricter than Cock Canary and his chicks, but they was more like real people an all. More human. Like firing guns were so important there weren't no time for being too nasty with it.

'Tight,' one of them keeps saying to me. 'Hug it like it's your sweetheart. The tighter you hold her, the more she'll love you.'

I tried. Pulled the thing right into my shoulder, but it weren't easy. For one thing, lying there weren't so good for my leg. And for the other thing, I was scared. Don't mind admitting. Of course it were exciting. The amount of time we'd carried that Smelly round, cleaned it, and cleaned it again. We was all dead excited to be shooting it at last. But after all we'd been told about the noise, and the kickback into your shoulder, and that if we didn't look after it proper, it'd blow up in your face. My hands was sticky.

The order to fire was drowned out straight off by the sound of everyone else shooting off.

I squeezed the trigger, and fired.

The noise was so loud in my ear that my grip slacked. The instructor was right. I should've held it tighter. The heavy wooden butt of that Smelly bashed into my shoulder like a jack hammer. It hurt so much my mouth fell open but no noise comed out. But I knowed I weren't the only one. All down the line, lads was yelling out. And it didn't get much better. Even though I did pull the stock in tight after that, my shoulder was already sore, so each shot still hurted it. On one side of me, Jim was doing okay. I think his strength meaned he could hold that thing steady as a rock. And of course the one person who didn't have no problem at all was Birdy. He was on my other side and grinned all the way through the afternoon. Never been so happy.

'Good shooting,' the instructor said to Birdy, after he'd been down the range checking how we'd got on. 'Let's hope you're as good with a live target.'

As luck would have it, Birdy saw a chance to show that he was. Even as the words was coming out of the instructor's mouth, a pigeon flapped up from the trees behind the target range. Birdy didn't need an invitation. His gun comed up to his shoulder, nice and tight, and he let off a round before any of the rest of us seed what was going on. Even the instructor flinched.

The pigeon dropped like a stone. We all cheered. Couldn't help ourselves. Only the instructor weren't so pleased, and started shouting.

'What in heck do you think you're playing at, you stupid little man!' He said, right in Birdy's face.

'You're on a charge. Discharging a weapon without orders.'

Birdy's smile dropped, and everyone else went quiet. The instructor shook his head, and turned to walk off.

'Nice shot though, lad,' he said.

17. TRAIN CRASH

It were a bit more than two weeks before we was finally marked as efficient for sending to the Front. But when it happened at last, there weren't no leave or nothing to celebrate it. As soon as we'd packed up everything an cleaned our tent, we made our way to the Quartermaster's stores, and was issued with one hundred and twenty rounds for each man an a groundsheet. That groundsheet were rubberised, which meant it were good for keeping the rain out if you wore it over the top of your service dress kit and tied it at the front.

'Uh oh,' says Sadsack, as we queued up at the rail depot. 'Canary alert.'

My eyes shifted. The three Canaries was marching straight towards us. I took in a breath and stayed still as I could. We was leaving the Territorial Infantry Camp, there weren't nothing else they could do. Or shouldn't be. But I knowed 'em better than that.

'Well, if it isn't the sooty engineers,' Cock Canary says, staring straight at me. 'Off to fight the Hun.'

Everyone else cheered, like they was glad to be off to take on the Germans. The Canary's face was like stone, and the Chicks' an all. In truth, I reckon the lads was cheering 'cause we was leaving them Canaries behind, going to war. And I reckon them Canaries was looking so stern 'cause they wasn't going. They was soldiers who'd never face the enemy. They knowed what we all thinked of 'em for that. But Cock Canary had one last little surprise for us.

'Before you go,' he says. 'I've just come to let you know that one of you lovely Privates has been selected to be 2 Section's new Section Leader. Now ATTENTION!'

'Private Arkell,' he shouts, looking at me then Jim. 'You're going to be thrilled. Both of you.'

My heart sinked. We hadn't had a Section Leader since Corporal Simpson went, but I knowed from Cock Canary's face, me an Jim wasn't going to be thrilled at all.

I were right. Adams appeared behind the Canaries. He had a white stripe on his arm. He was to join our Section, as a lance corporal. I seed Birdy's face. Every muscle in it went stiff, all at once. But Adams' face was straight. No sign of his usual glinting eyes.

'I don't want no trouble,' he says to Birdy, an to Jim an all, when we was squashed into the train wagon. 'Just want to do my job proper, that's all.'

Birdy nodded to him, an that were that. Jim just looked blank, like he didn't care either way.

I didn't get it, and was half expecting Adams to flare up any minute and give us what for. But he didn't.

'He ain't never had a proper position before,' Birdy says to me, after we found a corner of the carriage to ourselves. 'Never been trusted an that. We'll just have to see if he sticks to it.'

*

That train ride took forever. It weren't like any train I was used to seeing at the works. We was in a cattle truck, an it stinked just like you'd imagine a cattle truck stinked. And I reckon it was the slowest train that ever sat on a pair of rails. In normal days, Jim would've gone on an on about what sort of locomotive was pulling it, and about its steam efficiency and bogies an all. But he were still in his silent mood. I couldn't be bothered to try to talk to him.

One thing about that train being so slow though, was that we was able to get off and walk alongside it here an there, if our Section Leader said we could. Stretch our legs. And Adams seemed fine about that, probably 'cause he wanted to get off himself. We couldn't get away from the stink of cattle, mind. It were on us by then, right into our clothes.

When we got to where we was going, which maybe took two days or so, it were like all Hell broke out. Our wagon doors was thrown open, and we could see men everywhere, and more trains and motor lorries an horses. Everything on the move, with orderlies and corporals and sergeants all over, shouting an marking things on clipboards.

'Right you bleeders,' shouts Adams at 2 Section, his first chance to give orders. 'Get that kit together. Ready to disembark. Snap to it!'

'He'll go far, that begger,' whispers Birdy, helping me with my pack. 'He already thinks he's a Sergeant Major.'

We got our kit sorted, helping each other. We was wearing our greatcoats an groundsheets over everything. Ready to go. Except in the army things didn't always turn out the way you thinked they would. I reckon we stood on that train for near on four hours, waiting. None of us knowed what we was waiting for, but at least we was half entertained by Adams getting all worked up by it. Reckon with his new importance, he figured he should be told. Of course, nobody told him nothing. He may've had a white stripe, but in the end he were just another Tommy like the rest of us. Funny thing was, it were better having Adams trying to be all important, giving orders an that. Better than his normal bullying ways at least.

'You lot ain't the Camerons,' an orderly sticked his head in an said.

Adams said no we weren't, we was the Wiltshires, and tried to find out what was going on. The man just made a note on his clipboard and trotted off, didn't even answer.

After a few more false hopes like that, another bloke appeared. We all thought maybe our turn had comed at last, though none of us really thought it had. Well, I didn't anyway. My bad leg were aching, just from all that standing still. Then another man appeared, an officer, an shouted at the orderly.

'Get those men off there, NOW!'

The orderly straight off turned to shout at us. He didn't need to bother. Even before his mouth opened, Adams was on us, shouting an bellowing, and pushing at us to get off.

We didn't need to be told twice. There were a rush for the door, and men jumped down onto the tracks. In the push, I got squeezed between two others and lost my balance. As I landed, my leg gave way and I stumbled and fell between the tracks. For a moment I were just lying there, on a railway sleeper. A flash of remembering went through my head and the feeling of panic was like someone punched me in the belly. I twisted my face up, and there was Jim. He was looking down at me, but his face was blank. I thought he were going to stop and help me up. He didn't. Just stepped past me. Before I were able to think another thing, the orderly was there.

'On your feet,' he shouts, grabbing my webbing straps and tugging me up. 'Quick!'

He shoved me off the tracks, and I stood up an stared back. The others were all pouring off the wagon, some of them stumbling same as I done. I looked for Jim, but spotted something else instead. Then I got why the officer were in such a hurry for us to get off. Another train was coming. The tracks I'd jumped onto was shaking under its weight. I tugged my groundsheet an pack off, and rushed back to help pull our lads away. Some of the others was doing the same. We was going so fast, it wouldn't take us long to get everyone clear. Only a few was left on the train an Adams was there, hurrying them along an all. It were just as well. The front of the locomotive was almost blocking out the light, a huge black boiler coming right at us. It didn't look like it had any thoughts of stopping.

'Come on,' yelled Adams, jumping down and tugging one of the last men down with him. 'Get a ruddy move on.'

I helped to pull the other man away and Adams turned back. The second loco was there. I could feel its fumes stinging the back of my throat. There was only one bloke left on the wagon. Sadsack.

'What are you waiting for?' Shouts Adams, and we all starts shouting an all.

But there weren't no time. Birdy grabbed Adams's pack and yanked him towards the rest of us, an we all shouted to Sadsack to stay where he was. Only, as the locomotive came in, he either didn't hear us, or he reckoned he could still make it.

There weren't no sound of anything. Nothing what could be heared over the locomotive, anyhow. The noise of steam pistons pumping them huge black wheels round, and their squealing along the greasy tracks.

We all standed back, and let the train go on its way. It took a while. Maybe three or four minutes for all the wagons to pass, full of other men like us. But Sadsack weren't there when it'd gone. Just a splash of blood across a sleeper. The same one I'd been lying on.

'Lance Corporal,' shouted the officer at Adams. 'Get these men out of here, we haven't got all day.'

Then he shouted at the orderly as he marched off.

'And send a detail to clean the mess off the front of that locomotive.'

18. THE LETTER

Marching through France were much the same thing as marching anywhere else. Salisbury Plain, Basingstoke, the Territorial Infantry Camp. Left, right. Left, right. Same view as always. The pack of the bloke in front. Only thing what changed sometimes was the road underfoot. Mostly it were just mud, like we was used to, but for some of them miles we was taken down long straight roads made of cobbles, with tall trees all alongside. Them roads wasn't flat neither. High in the middle, and sloping down to the gutters each side, making it hard to march on if you was on the left or right flank of the column. Luckily, Birdy swapped with me so I could be in the middle.

Only other thing what was different, was that there weren't no Sadsack.

Fifty minutes marching. Ten minutes rest. Hour

after hour, from early morning right into the evening. Each hour as we set off, we felt good, with a cup of tea and maybe food inside us. Then as we marched along, the packs got heavier an heavier, them straps cutting into your shoulders, ammo packs an webbing an that weighing you down. Whether it were dry or raining, you still get to feel hot an itching inside that uniform. By the time rest period comed round again, you felt like you couldn't walk another step. I were glad to sit down and take my boots off.

'My feet ain't made for this,' Birdy says, giving his toes a rub. 'How're you doing Jimmy?'

I watched to see if Jim were going to answer, but there weren't nothing. Birdy looked at me and raised his eyebrows and shrugged.

'He's a sulky sod,' he says. 'That brother of yours. How are your plates, Noggin?'

I laughed. Plates of meat. What we called feet, learned from soldiers from London.

'Not too bad,' I smiled back. 'Few blisters. Bit of swelling up.'

Birdy leaned forward, and whispered at me, his ears sticking out from under his cap comforter.

'Any good for footie?'

That wiped the smile right off my face.

'What d'you bring that up for?' I asked, dropping my eyes so I didn't have to look at him.

'It's alright mate,' Birdy says, shifting himself so he's sitting right next to me. 'Everyone knows it weren't your fault.'

'Is that true?' I asked, looking at him. 'Has Jim telled 'em what happened.'

'He don't need to. It's them Canaries we all blame.'

'Then why is Jim being like he is, then?' I asked, and I heared my voice getting louder an higher. 'It's like he's angry with me. But it were him what didn't put no oil in the Major's bike. I don't know about them things.'

'You know what he's like,' Birdy says, squeezing my arm. 'His nose is all out of joint on account of getting it wrong. An engineering thing. Dented pride an that, but he'll get over it. He'll be back to normal soon enough. You see if he ain't.'

I weren't sure I believed what Birdy said, but it were nice to hear it all the same. I seed Adams coming along, so pulled my boots back on. It weren't easy, what with my feet being a bit puffy an all. But when Adams reached us I realised it weren't the end of the rest period yet. Adams had some mail for 2 Section.

'Arkell,' he shouted after he'd given out a few other letters.

He chucked one towards me. It was a bit bigger than most, and fatter an all.

'That should be for my brother,' I says, picking it up and heading towards Jim. 'He reads ours.'

Jim looked up. For a second, I thinked I seed some light in there.

'Just read the envelope, Arkell,' says Adams before shouting out the next name.

I did as he told me. Private Nicholas Arkell, 2 Section, 4 Platoon, B Company, it said. In neat writing that wasn't joined-up. That was me. I held it out in front of me and gawped at it, turning it over in my hands. I looked around, expecting someone to pop up any second and say there'd been a mistake. Was there a different Nicholas Arkell? Or it were really meaned for Jim, James Arkell. But the only voice were Adams again, shouting that it were time to get back on the march. We all jumped to it, of course, an I shoved the letter into my tunic pocket. Back into the ranks an back on the road.

That were the longest fifty minutes of my life. And the shortest. I couldn't stop thinking of that letter. I knowed the writing on the envelope weren't Mam's. It weren't Dad's, that's for sure. I couldn't think who would be writing to me, or what for. That meaned half the time we was going along I were thinking it would be good, and I were excited. A grin on my face that nobody could miss if they choosed to look. The other half of the time, I felt full of dread. A sick feeling right down in my belly. But I didn't even notice the weight of my pack, or the prickly heat or my boots. Or even my bad leg.

The moment we was given rest orders, I chucked down my pack and took myself off next to one of them tall French trees.

Emma Deacon. Emma Deacon was writing to me. A whole letter, and a pair of knitted gloves an all.

There was writing on both sides of the paper, all neat like the envelope. And I seed her name, clear as you like, at the end. Of course, ten minutes weren't enough time for me to read the rest, with my reading skills. Or lack of 'em. Them two years I spent getting better after my fall, laid on that sleeper bed, I never went to school. Later, when I did go, it weren't easy. For one thing I were in pain a lot of the time. Even sitting at a desk were hard. For another thing, I were in school with kids two years younger than me. I spent the whole time feeling like I was with babies, an wishing I could be with others my own age. Or with Jim. Besides, I weren't interested in what them teachers wanted me to learn, all in readiness for the railways. I weren't going into them works no matter what they all thought. Mam said if I'd been to school proper, for them two years, I would've been the smartest of 'em all, an could've done whatever I wanted to do. Still could. That's why she called me a little brainbox. Her little Noggin.

The only good thing I reckon, about school, was that I got to be in the same class as Emma Deacon.

When rest was over an we was called back to the ranks, I hadn't had no tea, no food, no water. Just sat there under that French tree with my hands out in front of me, staring at them gloves and imagining I were back under my wild cherry tree. It were the shortest ten minutes of my life. And the longest.

*

For two more days and nights we made our way towards the war proper. Most the time things carried on as normal. Marching, rest, marching again. Except now I had my new gloves on. Wool, they was, in different coloured stripes. Soft an warm. And we could hear guns now an all. Of course, the stomp of thousands of boots softened it some, along with them horse drawn wagons and motor lorries that comed after us. Not at night, though. We didn't have proper camps set up, no tents or nothing, and then the booming of them big guns seemed to go on the whole time with the sky glowing red and orange. We was so tired though, we still slept. Some of the time anyhow.

But it weren't always the guns what woke me up in them nights. Pictures filled my head. Mam coughing. Jim angry. Sadsack about to jump. In my mind,

Sadsack were screaming an covered in blood, and that officer was standing there shaking his head an calling him a mess.

Each day was taking us closer to the Front, of course. Soon, we seed the Front coming back to meet us.

'Off the road, you lot,' shouts a sergeant, striding down the column. 'Clear the way.'

It weren't rest time, but we did as we was told to, happy to take the extra break. Another column were headed towards us, and Birdy rolled himself a fag and lit it up as they passed us.

'Lucky bleeders,' he says. 'Reckon they must be on their way home.'

He might've been right, about them going home, anyhow. But not about 'em being lucky. As they comed closer we could see they was all injured one way or another. At first a load of ambulances drove past, then it were the walking wounded. Right there in front of us, men with bandages wrapped around their head, or body, or an arm, or both arms. In some cases, where arms used to be but weren't no more. Then came a great long column of men with bandages round their faces, covering their eyes. Every one of 'em shuffling along, holding on to the shoulder of the bloke in front.

'Gas,' I heared someone say. 'Blinded with gas.'

'Them Hun animals,' says Birdy. 'Using gas against our boys. That ain't soldiering. That's just plain evil.'

I breathed soft. My stomach feeled something I ain't feeled before. It was a sick feeling what gived me the shivers at the same time. Made me almost feel cold. But it weren't seeing the wounds that made me feel it. It was the men themselves. They didn't look up, even though lots of our lads was cheering 'em as they went by. Their eyes stayed down on the ground in front of them, one step at a time. The last part of the column was filled with men on crutches, or leaning on mates. Some of 'em had two crutches, some one. Some of 'em had two legs, some one. As they comed close to where I was stood, one bloke shuffled himself on his crutches towards us a bit. He lifted his head an looked straight at me. I couldn't tell how old he were. Young. Maybe young as me, maybe older. But there weren't nothing in that face. Nothing what I could recognise, nor understand. Black eyes staring at something no other body could see.

The cheering behind me stopped, and it feeled like my breathing did an all. I taked my eyes down from that empty stare, and seed the man's legs. Or what were left of 'em. One was gone. Just a stump wrapped in bandage. The other was half covered with a tatty trouser leg an dark stains. The foot were bare. No sock, no boot. Just black mud and sores.

I looked up again and quizzed the man's face. There weren't no answer, but I didn't need one. Without a thought, I dropped down an took my own boot off. The one on my bad leg. The man heaved himself off again, not interested in me or what I were up to. I hopped after him, and grabbed his shoulder.

'Here you go mate,' I says, tying the boot laces to one of his crutches. 'Don't know if it's the right size, but try it on at your next rest period.'

19. COMING CLEAN

Laundry time didn't happen too often in the army. Baths was even rarer. I reckon the army figured we was dirty little beggars anyhow. No point wasting good water on us. So we was dead excited when we arrived at a rest camp and seed there was baths there.

The camp were an old farm, about five or six miles behind our trench lines, we was telled. It had a load of barns and a brick built house an all. Apart from that it weren't much like a farm no more. Cattle was replaced with men. Now it were typical army, with the stink of stale sweat and incinerators burning rubbish day an night. Mud everywhere, with rotted duck boards as the only way to get around on it. But we weren't complaining none.

My feet was sore, of course. But I weren't the only one. After I gave my boot to the one legged man, I took off the other one an all, and shoved it in my

146

pack, to balance me up some. As it happened, the road weren't that bad in my socks. A mud track, but well pressed down by all them feet that had marched down it. Soft and giving. At the next rest period, Jim comed up to me. He didn't say nothing. Just gived me his boots, and nodded. I tried to give 'em back, but he hushed me up, pointing out that Adams were on the hunt for something to have a go about. Giving my boot away would be a chargeable offence, so I shut up and slipped Jim's boots on. They was way too big of course, but that didn't matter none. They feeled like Heaven. Getting back into ranks, the other lads made sure Jim was tucked away in the centre. Out of sight. His feet at least.

Then, at the next break, something odder happened. One of the other blokes came up to me and gived me his boots, taking Jim's from me and giving 'em back to Jim. Without a word being spoke. Same at the next break an all, a different lad. And the next.

When we reached the camp, my feet was sore, but only 'cause of wearing different sized boots all the while. I didn't care none though, and cheered along with all the others when we was queued up outside the bath house.

Stripping off was a pleasure, sort of. Even though it weren't exactly warm, it weren't cold neither. But it were so good to get out of that dirty, itchy tunic an them trousers. I tied mine up in a bundle with my dog tags and handed 'em over. As I moved along the line, I could see the men getting into the baths. They looked like bleaching vats, big an grey, and was being constantly topped up by men bringing hot water from a row of boilers. It were then I realised we was expected to take everything off. Really everything. Shirt, socks. Pants even. And that weren't the worst of it. Them what was taking the clothes away weren't other soldiers. They was girls. French girls, been taken on to do the laundry. They was giggling and laughing at all them soldiers with not a stitch on 'em. Of course I had no choice but to do the same. I'm sure I were bright red, from top to muddy toe.

My worries stopped though when I seed Sergeant Hodson. He were there an all, starkers as the day he were born, and all the way down the outside of his right leg was a bright red wheal. A scar as long as my arm, knarly and hairless.

'Shrapnel wound from the last war,' he says to me, as a tub comed free. 'But a bad leg doesn't stop you from being a good soldier, does it now?'

I looked up and he was staring right into my eyes. He tapped the side of his nose, and winked.

'Go on then,' he nodded towards the empty tub. 'In you jump.'

Once I were in that bath I didn't care about

nothing no more, and sang along with all the others. Even when it were done and they hosed us down with cold water to wash off the suds.

'These socks is useless,' I says to Birdy as we was given different underwear from the laundry. 'They ain't even big enough to cover my big toe.'

'That's nothing,' he says back. 'Look at your brother.'

I looked up and Jim was standing there looking down at himself. He was wearing a pair of pants that looked more like a tent. So big he was having to hold 'em up, and so baggy I couldn't help thinking of Auntie Jean's drawers hanging on the line in our yard back home.

'Can you imagine the size of the bloke who wore 'em before,' Jim muttered, shaking his head.

I looked at my huge brother standing there in nothing but them pants.

'He must've been a giant,' I says.

'Or had the biggest arse in the British army,' says Birdy, grinning.

Jim's face cracked a smile. Then he laughed, and so did the rest of us.

*

A whole tin of pork an beans for each of us seemed like a feast. Especially as there was lumps of French bread to be had an all. In truth, the meat in them tins weren't nothing worth really talking about. Lost in the beans really. But it were hot, and we was past caring now the marching was done and we was clean, even if that new underwear itched from the disinfectant they boiled it in.

Jim passed me my tin and we climbed up into our bunking space. It were a makeshift wooden platform built into a barn. In all there was four or five floors, each with about two dozen men on, stacked up one above the other. The whole lot shaked every time someone moved.

'I've been useless, Noggin,' my brother says. 'I know no amount of saying sorry is going to make up for it.'

He spooned in another mouth of beans.

'First I try to make life as miserable for you as I'm able. Then I can't keep my mouth shut, and get us into trouble with the Canaries. Then...'

The spoon hangs in front of his mouth. I want to remind him about lying about Mam. But I keep quiet, figuring there weren't much point. Finally he speaks, real soft like.

'...the motorbike oil.'

'It's alright, Jim,' I says back. 'Birdy told me. No-one blames me for the football an that. It's them Canaries. Cock Canary. His fault.'

'No, Noggin. That ain't the point. I'm your big

brother and I'm supposed to be looking after you. Instead, I let you take the blame for something that was down to me. I was too wrapped up in my own thinking. How could I not put oil in that bike? So stupid.'

I scraped around the bottom of my tin, and digged out the last few beans. When I turned to look at Jim, his hands was limp, letting his tin go, and his face was hanged right down on his chest. His shoulders was shaking.

'Jim. Jim,' I says, twisting around to him, and making the platform wobble. 'It's alright. Honest. You don't need to worry none.'

'Oi!' Someone shouts. 'Keep still, you beggers.'

'But it ain't alright, Noggin,' Jim sobbed. 'It ain't at all. Don't you see?'

He looked me in the face, gripping me by the shoulders. Tears running down his face an them big hands pressing like vices. I almost had to hold my breath to stop from yelping out.

'I'm supposed to be an engineer. An apprentice,' he says, through gritted teeth. 'What will they say at the works when they found out what I've done? Even an idiot knows you can't run a machine without oil. What will Dad say?'

'Dad won't care about that none,' I tried to comfort him. 'He'll just care about you.'

Jim's face changed, paled.

'He doesn't care about me,' he says. 'He hates me.'

I weren't expecting that. Not at all. It took a few seconds before I were able to speak again.

'What,' I stutters. 'What are you going on about? Dad don't hate you. You two is thick as thieves. All the time, off gassing about railways an the works an everything. He never talks to me like that. Not ever.'

Jim didn't say nothing. He collapsed towards me, his hands relaxing an his head burying into my shoulder. I figured he were just upset, not seeing things clear.

We didn't say no more and after a bit, Jim shifted himself an went off to sleep. I weren't tired though. Besides, I had something I needed to do.

20. OLD FRIENDS

Emma Deacon. I must've read that letter a hundred times. More. I couldn't read it quick of course, but her lettering was so neat I were able to get through it all without any help from anyone. Which was good, 'cause I didn't want no one else to see it anyhow. Emma told me that all the girls was asked to write to a soldier, to cheer 'em up. And she choosed me. She knitted the gloves an all. I were determined to write back, no matter how long it taked.

In the end, my letter weren't as long as hers. But I did ask her how she was, and if she was having a nice time during the war. I told her about Adams being a Lance Corporal and my Mam being sick, an wondered if she might know that already. Or maybe even know if Mam was out of hospital or not. In her letter she also asked me if there were anything I needed. There was one thing I could think of. I weren't sure if it was the sort of thing she meant, or whether she could get it or not. But I writed it anyway.

Apart from that letter, I tried writing two others a week later. To Mam and Dad, of course, and another one to Emma, on account of getting plenty of rest time in that camp. At first anyways.

Of course, it weren't all nice in the camp. For one thing we all knowed we was dead close to the Front now. We could hear it a lot of the time. Artillery and machine guns an all, much louder than we'd ever heared before. Even so, we tried to enjoy ourselves, and our lads got to play football with a load of Welshmen from the next camp along. Jim didn't join in, mind. Although he'd said sorry to me an that, he still didn't proper come out of his silent mood. Not really. Just spent the time mooching about the place, or staring into nothing.

Birdy was the opposite. He spent all his time busy, mainly off hunting for things. At first it were just game. Rabbits an that. But after a bit he decided that weren't worth bothering with, on account of so many others hunting an all. Also, he still couldn't use his gun, else face a charge for 'losing' ammunition. So he switched to hunting better stuff. Like fags, or tins of peaches in syrup, an other things for trading. Even got himself a baccy tin what looked like it was made of silver. I don't know how he managed it, and I reckoned it were best not to ask. But I didn't care really, neither. Especially as one of the first things he turned up with was a pair of boots for me.

'Went up to the ambulance station in the village,' he told me. 'There was a whole pile outside it. All there for the taking.'

I didn't want to think about what that meaned. About what happened to the men who used to own them.

But them boots was a good fit, an that were enough for me. Especially as the rest breaks soon stopped. We gets to do more an more fatigues, an camp got real busy, with more and more men moving in, and the fields around us filling up with horses and vehicles an equipment. It weren't long before the whole area were bristling. We was all going to be part of the 'Big Push', we heard others whispering.

The barn platform finally collapsed under the weight of all them men. We was lucky, out on bucket fatigues when it happened. Two men was luckier still, and got sent back to Blighty, England, 'cause of injuries they got when the thing fell on 'em.

'Jocks,' says Birdy, as another load of troops arrived. 'Back from the Firing Line, I reckon.'

He were right. The Scots was just back from a two week stint in the Firing Line trenches. I couldn't help thinking they was actually quite smartly turned out.

Considering. They was all wearing kilts like Edward Macpherson had been back at the Territorial Infantry Camp, which meaned they got called Kilties, as well as Jocks an that. And they had a side cap instead of a cap comforter like us, and seemed to be wearing shoes instead of boots. Heavy brogues. They got just as muddy as our boots, mind.

Of course, they weren't the first men we seed back from the trenches. There was some almost every day we'd been there. Usually though, they was support troops. Men who'd been ferrying stuff up to the Firing Line, or lying in wait in the trenches behind, in case they was needed. We hated it when they turned up. For one thing, they always went to the front of the queues for everything. First for food an drink. First for baths. And they was first for choosing fatigues an all, which meaned we got all the dirty jobs, like slopping out, or ferrying bales of laundry backwards an forwards, in the slippery mud.

'Right you lot,' says Adams one morning at breakfast. 'We're to help the Jocks in setting up a new camp. The whole Company. So pay attention at parade.'

We did as he told us, and after parade we marched off to the fields nearby. The place were full of engineers staking out marker posts, and there was convoys of lorries an wagons full of kit, which we was to unload and move to where we was told. 4 Platoon was put under a Scottish Sergeant Major. We couldn't hardly understand his accent, but he seemed alright. Better than them Canaries back at Territorial Infantry Camp anyhow. He reminded me of Edward Macpherson, and the other Scots what had stayed with us at the beginning of the war. Only person who didn't like him was Adams. That made me like him even more.

'Grief,' I says to Birdy, as we carried a bundle of tent poles along. 'How big is this camp gonna be, Birdy? It goes on forever.'

'You're not wrong there, Noggin. Bloomin' huge, is all I can say.'

We made our way down one of the newly laid frog board roads. Tents was going up in all directions. Far as the eye could see.

'You're right lads,' says a voice. 'One of the biggest in France.'

Me an Birdy both turned, and seed an officer there. A Scottish Lieutenant, in his kilt an all. We dropped the poles and saluted. Then I grinned. It was Edward.

He laughed, then introduced himself to Birdy, shaking his hand like a proper gentleman. Birdy's eyes looked like they was going to pop out.

'Come on you two. You can come back for those

poles later,' Edward says, striding off. 'I have a special delivery that I need two soldiers to help me with. Swiss chocolate!'

*

First hint we got that we might be ready for the off was oranges and chestnuts. I hadn't ever had an orange before, and chestnuts only at Christmas. I loved the way the orange juice trickled all over you. I didn't like peeling it, mind. Or how the juice got all sticky after.

'This ain't good, you know,' Adams tells the Section, slinging aside his peel. 'It can only mean one thing. Fattening us for the slaughter. The Front.'

I hadn't heared Adams talk like that before. His green eyes seemed to lose some of their sparkle. For a moment I reckoned he were proper afraid about going to the Front. Of course, he soon snapped out of it.

'Time for you useless lot to do some proper soldiering,' he says.

We all knowed he was right. For one thing, there weren't no more rest times. More combat training, more fatigues, more everything. Especially gas mask practice. We spent ages pulling on an off them canvas bags with their thick glass eyeholes. Tube Helmets they called 'em, to protect us from the evil Hun's dirty gas attacks. We called 'em rubbish sacks, and they stinked like that an all. An evil, chemical smell that made you want to retch.

In the distance there was more an more of them explosions an gunfire. At night all I could do was lay there an listen. Next to our camp, the area we helped to set up turned out to be a field hospital. The area was covered with white tents, all carrying the red cross and filled with trestle tables an medical supplies. Standing there, ready. And long deep ditches with sacks of lime rowed up alongside 'em. We all knowed what they was waiting for.

'Knobs,' says Birdy one day. 'I seed a dozen or more going up to the farmhouse in them fancy cars. Red collar tabs, every one of 'em. Colonels, maybe Generals.'

Then the rain started, and the order we'd all been waiting for comed.

21. FIVE CHANCES

Our Colonel was too far off for me to hear all of what he were saying. I weren't that bothered. We was all mustered, the whole Battalion, maybe five or six thousand of us, but the shuffling of all them men an the pitter patter of the rain made it hard to pay attention. But I did get some of it. The Wiltshires was heading to the Front, the Colonel said, along with two Welsh battalions and the Camerons, which was Edward's regiment. We was to join the Frenchies for the 'Big Push' and drive the Hun out of the local coal mining areas, an all the way back to Prussia. Then he prattled on about new honours for the regiment, and telling that we mustn't stick our bayonets in too far, else we might not get 'em out again. And other nonsense. The only thing we really needed to know was that we was marching that afternoon. By night time, we'd be in the trenches.

'I've been working it out,' says Birdy, as we got our kit ready. 'I reckon the odds is stacked in our favour. For starters, we've got God on our side, ain't we? And our guns is way better than theirs.'

He held his Smelly up to his shoulder and looked down its shiny sights.

'And we're better shots an all.'

To our surprise, Jim then spoke up. Me an Birdy and a few others all turned to hear what he had to say.

'Five chances,' he says, slowly tying his bootlaces.

Then he stopped and looked up at us. His face was set dead stern.

'Think about it,' he says, his eyes flicking from one to the other of us. 'You might get killed, of course. Everyone knows that. But maybe you'll get taken prisoner and sit out the war eating German sausages, or get wounded and sent back to Blighty. Home.'

He looked down and gave a final tug on his lace, then looked back at us again.

'Or you'll just go barmy. Bonkers. Mad as a hatter. And if that happens, you won't care anyhow.'

I was counting off the chances on my fingers, as he were telling 'em. Killed, prisoner, wounded or mad. I had one finger left up. Jim leaned towards me and bends it down, looking me in the eye.

'Or maybe you'll come out in one piece. Won't

even get a scratch,' he says.

It all went quiet after that. There weren't much else to be said. We had one hour to write a last letter to our loved ones. Mine were to Mam an Dad, and it were short, of course. I stuffed it in my pocket. I looked at Jim. He were staring into space, biting the end of his pen. Then he let out a puff of air and shook his head, stuffing his bit of paper into a pocket an all.

I looked at him and caught his eye. I tried to smile. Then we had to join the ranks.

We leaved behind our greatcoats an packs, loading 'em onto wagons. I shifted my haversack round to my back, an tied the cord of my groundsheet round my neck, making it like a raincoat. We was all issued with 180 extra rounds, which was heavy. Birdy didn't care though.

'All the more for the Hun,' he says.

He weren't so happy when we was given our rations mind. As well as full water canteen and our iron rations we got a lump of bread and an extra piece of cheese, an a tin of cold pea soup. It was only after they gived us that lot that we was told the Company cookers weren't coming with us. What we was carrying was all we was going to get, and we wasn't to touch any of it on the march, not even the water. Birdy cussed.

Last of all, I strapped on the bag with that stinky

gas mask hood. We was set. Full Battle Order.

'Do me proud lads,' says Sergeant Hodson, marching alongside as we rowed up ready for the off.

I smiled at him. Then the smile dropped. He weren't in Full Battle Order, just his normal uniform.

'Sorry to say I ain't coming with you, chaps,' he carries on, an I can see he don't want to catch nobody's eye. 'On account of what the Boers did to my old leg.'

With that, he slapped his right leg. The command for the column to march were given, and Sergeant Hodson stood to attention an saluted us. I stared at him as we slowly shuffled off.

'Eyes front!' He ordered, an I think he winked at me.

The Scots led the way, with their pipers. The officers was up the front an all, on their well groomed horses. Reckon they thought bagpipe music was a good thing to lead us into battle with. Though it weren't that easy to hear it with the stomp of boots an rain splashing on all them groundsheet raincoats. At one point, I did hear an engine though, an turned to see. It were Major Cromwell, riding alongside the column on his Douglas motorcycle.

Jim was ahead of me, covered with his groundsheet, same as everyone else. I only knowed it were him 'cause of his height. I couldn't reach him without breaking ranks.

'Jim,' I says, trying to get his attention without Adams hearing me. 'Jim. It's the Major, on his bike. It's alright. Look.'

But Jim's head didn't move. He didn't hear me, or didn't care.

I didn't bother talking after that. Nor did anyone else much. We seed metalled roads, but them wasn't for us. The roads we went on was mud and gravel mostly. Tarmac were only for moving the big guns, behind them massive steam tractors. I were in the middle of the column, so could only peak past the other lads from under my groundsheet hood. When I did, left or right, I seed columns of other men like us, on the march, or long lines of wagons and mules with ammo crates an packs an that. There were even a light railway shunting stuff all over, just like the works back home.

Being mining country there was spoil heaps an all. Huge black hills stretching from left to right up ahead of us. That was where the Hun was digged in we was told. Off to our right, a long ways off, there was the black iron towers of a double mining shaft. Everyone reckoned it looked like Tower Bridge in that London.

We had to march through a store depot, full of wooden planks what looked like railway sleepers, an piles of sandbags, and artillery shells, and wooden spools wrapped with barbed wire or communications cables. Everything was sitting in mud an them duck boards was slippy as Hell.

Every now and then we'd hear an explosion go off. After a bit, near dusk, I could see 'em an all, above the heads of them in front. A flash then a load of dirt lifting into the air. Smoke and flames turning the sky orange and black. Every time one of them shells came down I felt my shoulders flinch, and my eyes shut down tight. It would all go quiet for a moment. Part 'cause the noise made you deaf. Part 'cause you stopped still, checking you was still alive before moving on again.

As the light faded more, everything got slower an slower. The traffic coming down from the Line got as busy as us going up. Ambulances, walking wounded, supplies an that. Sometimes we was taking just one step then waiting ages before the next one. At one point we stopped altogether an stood there for what must've been about an hour. It weren't good for my leg. The stiffness was nagging away something rotten. But I knowed everyone else's legs was probably aching an all.

Word came down the column that some Military Policemen wouldn't let the Battalion move on account of our colonel not having the right permit. Jim shaked his head.

'We must be getting close,' says Birdy, pointing.
'Look.'

Ahead of us against the dull grey sky I seed
balloons up in the air. Observation balloons. Under
the one nearest us, I could make out its basket
hanged below, and the dark shape of a man watching
out over the enemy lines. He looked small an lonely
up there. An easy target for the Hun. I were glad I
was down on the ground, an surrounded by others.

After a bit, my bad leg felt something changing.

'Birdy,' I says. 'We's going down.'

'Support trenches,' he said back, all matter of fact.

Slowly, the road sloped down and got narrower.
Adams shouted to us to close ranks. Soon there was
piles of sandbags along each side. Then we was right
down in a trench proper, an we was walking below
normal ground level, with the only light coming from
covered candle holders and the dull sky above. Them
tight walls made me think of sneaking along the
backsies behind our house. Only there weren't no
door into our yard nor Mam waiting with supper on
the table. The column slowed again. It was crowded
an dark, but Adams's voice was still clear as a bell.

'2 Section,' he says. 'We're to join the Scots in the
Firing Line. Follow the man in front.'

Jim were the man in front of me, and Birdy behind
me. All I could see was Jim's broad back and the rain

hoods of the rest of our Section just in front of him. So I just follows, like Adams telled us. I can't say how long we carried on for, or how far we went. The trenches kinked and twisted so if a shell landed it weren't able to do so much damage round all them corners. The walls was made up of wooden shoring or corrugated iron sheets, an mud, of course. All the way we was passing men, some busy with something, some just sitting there, smoking an that.

Voices shouted that we was near the Firing Line. It gave me a lump in my throat to think that after that there weren't nothing. Just the empty space called no-man's land. Then them giant slag heaps, hiding the German trenches. The Hun. Fritz. The enemy we'd come to kill. Out there, just a matter of yards from where we was. Waiting to kill us.

Word got passed back that the Firing Line trench weren't as deep as the support trenches, so we was to take care to keep our heads down. Jim had to almost double himself up. I followed him through a small gap in the sandbags an across a little platform made of wooden crates.

'Come on,' snaps Adams, waving us through. 'We ain't got all day.'

Then I heared a whistling noise, and Jim crashed back into me.

22. INTO THE FIRING LINE

I pushed back against my brother, but I didn't have no chance of shifting that weight. If it weren't for the lads behind me, I would've been squashed flat in the bottom of the trench.

'What you doing?' I shouts. 'Get off me.'

Slowly, Jim pulled himself away, and him an some others shoved something to one side and clambered across the crates. As I got my breath back an followed 'em, I seed what it was they'd moved. It were one of our lads. His face was looking at me, familiar as ever. Except one of his eyes was just a black hole, with something dark an shiny trickling out from it. And he weren't moving none.

'Hurry it up Noggin,' Birdy shouts at me, even though his voice seemed a long way off.

I felt a tug on my arm. Adams pulled me across the crates.

'Come on,' he says. 'Move yourself. Head down.'

I slid off the crate platform and into the mud at the bottom of the trench. The walls of the Firing Line trench was shorter than me. Even with the piles of sandbags on top, on the parapet. I knowed I had to keep my head down like we was told to. I'd seen what happened if you didn't, but I tried not to think about it. Jim was almost on his knees, the rain splattering over his back.

We had to push our way through, on account of the place already being filled with troops, and it were bare wide enough for three or four men at any point. Them who was there already was Kilties, prattling at us in their funny accents as we moved past.

'Nice day for it, lads,' one says, an I could just about make out his smiling teeth in the dark. 'Shame about the weather.'

'Thanks for joining the party,' says another. 'We was starting to think we was going to have all them Fritzies to ourselves.'

Soon we slowed right down. Again. Birdy pushes me to the side and I found Jim and the others of 2 Section was stopped there already, in a space cut away into the back of the trench. The rest of the Battalion just pushed past us. Looking for their own spaces like passengers on a busy train carriage. Our area were just about big enough for us, with some of them Scottish Kilties leaning against the walls either side.

'Well, this is good a den as any,' says Birdy, getting out his baccy tin and rolling one up. 'Welcome to France, lads.'

I wanted to say something about what happened at the crates. One of our lads had been killed. But Birdy had other ideas. He stuck the ciggy in his mouth, an waved his hand for us to all come in close. When we was huddled about, he pulled a bottle from inside his groundsheet. He shows it to us, half hiding it behind one hand.

'Don't tell them bleedin' Jocks,' he whispers. 'But anyone fancy a gargle of whisky?'

'Where d'you get that from?' one of the lads asks.

Birdy just smiled, and tapped the side of his nose. Then he holded the bottle out to Jim. But Jim weren't having none of it, and turned away, shaking his head. Birdy just shrugged, put the bottle to his lips an took a slug. After the rest of 'em done the same, Birdy takes the bottle back an pushes it at me, holding it in front of my face.

'Come on Noggin,' he says. 'It'll warm you up.'

'Go on,' says the others.

I looked to Jim, but he weren't paying no heed, face hidden behind that dripping hood.

'Sod it,' I says, and grabbed the bottle.

I gawped at it for a second, an licked my lips. Then I takes a little look at Birdy. He was smiling so I just tipped the thing up and felt the whisky going into me. It were sharp and tasted like nothing I ever had before. Then I spluttered something silly, when I feels it burning the back of my throat. I grabbed my neck and bended forward, rasping. Birdy snatched the bottle off me, and laughed, an so did the others. Most of 'em anyway. Not my brother though.

'Looks like we've finally made a man out of Noggin,' Birdy says, taking another slug for himself.

Then we just stood there, talking away ten to the dozen like old women. I reckon I was the worst of all, going on about my boots, and how I liked whisky now, and Kilties an Edward Macpherson. I only shut up when I realised I'd spluttered out the name of Emma Deacon, and feeled my face flushing up. Them others was too busy talking amongst themselves to notice, I think. But I did see Jim's head turn, an caught a glimpse of his eye in the shadow of his hood. He didn't say nothing, mind. Which I were glad of.

'Anyone know what happened to Adams?' Someone asked. 'Weren't he behind us? Ain't seen him come past.'

The answer comed soon after. We heared him shouting, in that crystal clear voice of his.

'Arkell,' he was yelling. 'Private Arkell. Where the

heck are you, soldier?'

Me an Jim looked at each other. I couldn't see what he were thinking, but I reckon it were the same as me. *What now?* My belly cramped up.

Maybe he wouldn't spot us. With everyone hid under their groundsheets. But there weren't no way to hide Jim.

'There you are, you begger,' says Adams, as he spotted him. 'Parcel for you. Major Cromwell said to make sure you got it.'

That made everyone's faces pop out from under their hoods. Especially mine. Jim pulled his hood right off, an nearly standed up, clear taken by surprise. Luckily, Birdy grabbed his shoulder before he stuck his head above the parapet. Ripe for a German sniper. Adams throwed the parcel at him. It was wrapped in brown paper with string, and it were round. Jim held it and stared at Adams.

'For me?' He says. 'And the Major wanted me to have it?'

'If you ain't gonna open it, Arkell,' Adams snapped. 'I'll take it back. We need to be readying for the Push. Come on, we ain't got all day.'

'Yeah,' says Birdy. 'Come on. We all want to see.'

I leaned back against the mud wall, letting my face sink under my hood an smiling to myself. I reckon most could've guessed what it were, it weren't exactly difficult. I already knowed exactly what it was.

'It's a football,' says Jim, his eyebrows raised high an dripping in the rain.

It was a fine, leather football. Posted from the department store back home, McKilroy's. There was a note an all, wishing 'our brave lads' all the best. It was what I'd asked Emma Deacon for. Whether the shop had meaned to address it to Jim, or to me, I don't know. The label just said Private Arkell. It got to the right one anyhow, in a way. And the fact that Major Cromwell made sure it reached us, was like the icing on the cake. He clear didn't hold no grudge against Jim.

And Emma Deacon done it for me. That were the cherry on top.

There was shouting from up the trench, shifting everyone's thoughts from the ball. An officer comed through telling us we was to get out the way. He were carrying a lamp that lit up a red, green an white band on his arm. A Royal Engineer. A gas man. He were followed by others, carrying long metal pipes. They all had a big white patch on their back with a number on it. Two lads to each pipe an about twenty of 'em in all. But them pipes wouldn't fit round the corners of the trench, so was carried above their heads. We squashed to let 'em pass.

Then there was a flash an everything went bright

and hot, 'specially my face. I rocked back, stumbling against the side of the trench. When my eyes cleared a bit, I blinked and blinked, trying to see proper and rubbing at my face. It were tingling all over, and my ears was full of a buzzing noise an shouting.

Where there was a load of men a second ago, there was now just a gap and mud, obvious even in the dinginess. But the more I looked, the more things didn't make no sense. Then I realised it weren't just mud I were looking at. There was bits of men, and pipes, just lying there, some of 'em bent up. Men as well as pipes. The engineer officer came back, shouting orders.

'You there,' he says. 'Pick up those pipes. Quickly.'

I didn't think he were looking at me, so I just leaned against the muddy trench side and ducked my face back into my hood. Then I hears Adams. He were shouting at the top of his voice. I turned around and him and Jim was face to face.

'If I tells you to help the officer,' Adams was screaming. 'Then you ruddy well will.'

'I ain't doing it,' Jim shouted back, clutching the football to his chest. 'Going to shoot me are you?'

I grabbed at Jim's tunic sleeve and tried to pull him away, an down. Afraid he were going to stand up to full height. I'd seen my brother like this before, an I knowed what comed next. He were ready to explode. All his feelings, about the Major's bike, and the ball, and me. It was all bubbling up. If Mam had been there, she would've seen it coming too. Birdy were there like a shot an all, leaning forward to put himself between the two of 'em.

'It's alright,' he says to Adams. 'I'll do it. It's fine.'

Jim's face didn't flinch, just carried on staring at Adams. Adams looked at Birdy, then turned in my direction. For a second, me an him was staring straight at one another. His eyes was blazing green, even in that darkness. At first I thinked he were going to hit me.

'No,' he says, looking back at Jim, and ignoring Birdy altogether.

Then his hand snatched out like, and grabbed my shoulder strap. With all the strength of that wiry arm of his, he yanked me away from the trench wall.

'If you're not going to obey orders,' he shouted, looking at Jim still. 'Then cripple boy here can go instead.'

23. THE FINAL BARRAGE

Before Jim or me could say anything, Adams shoved me towards one of them pipes. I stumbled forward an the officer was on me in an instant, barking at me to pick the thing up from the mud. I turned to Birdy. He was gritting his teeth an shaking his head at Adams. Adams turned away.

'Don't worry Noggin,' Birdy shouts. 'You'll be fine mate. Keep your head down.'

The pipe was heavy. I'd hardly even got hold of it when the bloke lifting the other end was away, his number patch already off round the first corner. I could still hear Birdy shouting after me, and Jim an all, I think. But there weren't nothing to be done.

I went as quick as I could, hoping my leg weren't going to let me down none. But the trench weren't good for walking in. It got wetter and wetter, with the rain making muddy puddles all along. The officer kept ordering us to go quicker an that.

I tried stepping over them puddles or around 'em, but it weren't easy given all the men lining up along each side, and with trying to carry a pipe that was longer than two or three men end to end. And I still had my Smelly an everything an all. There were only just about room for us to squeeze through. Even then, the engineering officer had to shout to get people out of the way.

After a bit, I gave up on trying to miss the puddles. They was getting bigger 'til the trench floor was near covered with water, spilling over my boots and soaking into the puttees. Then I had that hot feeling start working its way up my leg.

I don't know how far we went, but I was flat exhausted and wet to the skin by the time we got to where we was going. I were lucky mind, my leg held out. And one of the other men got a bullet in his hand, where we was having to hold the pipes up so high.

'Put the pipes down over there,' the Royal Engineer officer says to us.

A load of other engineers came and took the pipes off us. Behind 'em I could see rows of big tall cylinders, standing all along the side of the trench. And there weren't hardly any men there neither. Just the engineers. One of 'em seed me staring.

'Chlorine gas, mate,' he says. 'We're going to give the Hun a taste of his own medicine. Them pipes is to deliver it to 'em.'

I looked at him, quizzing. Everyone said gas was evil, an now we was using it an all. If I could've thinked of something to say, I might've said it. But there weren't no time.

'You soldiers,' the officer says to me, and to the other men what helped bring the pipes. 'Back to your units. Double quick now, or you'll miss the Push.'

I didn't need to be told twice.

I ran fast as my stupid leg would let me, even though I had no idea how far 2 Section was, or when the Push might happen. In my head, I just keeped on saying I had to get back to the others. Jim an Birdy. They couldn't go into battle without me. They just couldn't.

My trenching tool bashed against my leg, and my boots was splashing muddy water over all them other men lining the trench, and they was shouting things at me. But I didn't care. Just kept running.

It weren't fast enough though, and every here and there, one of my feet would sink and the mud would grab it like, stopping me and making me cry out. Then something else went wrong with my foot. I were already limping 'cause of my bad leg, but this was something different. I looked down and both my feet was under the mud. I pulls one up, then the other an then I sees what the problem was.

'My boot,' I shouts out loud. 'My ruddy boot. Where's my boot?'

I swung round and splashed back some, reaching down and fumbling under the water. But I couldn't find it. It was stupid. My boot didn't matter none, and it weren't like I hadn't done without a boot before. But right there an then, it seemed like the most important thing in all the world. Tears was pushing up behind my eyes, an my heart were going like a steam train. I dropped to my knees, and thrashed left and right an all over. I had to find it. But it were almost pitch black down there at the bottom of the trench. In the end, I just kneeled there and slumped back on my heels, grabbing at my face with my mud covered hands.

'You alright, son?' One of the men nearby asked.

I looked up. His head was just a black shape against the dark sky, but I could tell his eyes was smiling. He reached out a hand. I don't know what I must've looked like to him.

'No,' I says, quiet like. 'No, I ain't.'

Then I heared my breathing speeding up and I gritted my teeth together.

'No I ain't bleedin' alright,' I shouted.

I bashed at the water with both hands curled into

fists, screaming as I did. And that were when I feeled something, there right in front of me. I scrabbled about and pulled it out. It was my boot. In a second, I were up again and shoving my foot into it, mud and water splurging over the top.

'Ha,' I says, pulling it on firm and looking at the man again.

Then I pushed him out of my way an carried on, fast as I were able. I only got a few hundred yards, probably not even that, before a boom made me throw myself down. All the blokes nearby did the same. But this weren't no loose shell from the Hun. Another boom followed, then another. I clasped my hands over my ears and feeled the ground shaking. It was our barrage, bombardment. Our heavy artillery was firing, letting rip with their massive howitzers. They weren't going to stop now, not until there weren't nothing left of the enemy's barbed wire an trenches, nor the Huns neither.

But even though we seed plenty of bombs an that going off in training, nothing they ever telled us made me ready for how it feeled to be in the middle of a barrage. The noise weren't like nothing else. You couldn't tell one blast from another, nor tell where the din was coming from or going to. It were everywhere, shaking over everything. Like you was living in a world made of sound. Buried inside a train boiler with a million steam riveters working nonstop all around you. Even when I clamped both arms round my head, it didn't make no difference, couldn't hardly feel any part of me. Except maybe my heart, which were fit to burst. Staring out, I seed a man looking at me. He was about thirty, or older. Badly shaved and with a square hard face. But he were white as chalk an his teeth was rattling.

In the middle of all that din, thoughts rattled around in my head. First they was just whispers, snatched thinkings here an there. Voices lost in the cannon fire. Then I heared what them voices was saying, and my heart leaped. This were the start of the Big Push. When them guns had done their job, it would be time for us. Over the top. Officers' whistles would be going off an we'd all be expected to cross no-man's land and finish things off.

I knowed that was how it worked. Done the assault training enough times. But I was in the wrong place, with strangers. Instead of with my own lads. 2 Section. Birdy. And Jim.

The noise screeched, and I thought my ears was going to bleed. But I pulled myself up to my feet, still remembering to keep my head down, and set off again, fast as my leg would let me. My heart was pumping faster than ever. I could feel the sweat running down inside my tunic.

As I pushed on, I noticed a change in the noise. A gap. Our own booming turned to a ringing in my ears, and I could hear the Hun firing back. Mortars an howitzers an that. Big stuff, small stuff, pip-squeaks. Chucking everything at us in return for ours, and filling the trench with burning smoke. But I knowed if I could hear the Hun artillery, our barrage was done.

I heared bells ringing next. In my head it was just like the warning bells back in the tunnel to the works. But there was something else an all. I could see the men around me. Make out their faces, all with a grey look. It were getting lighter. Morning. That made my stomach knot up. It was nearly time.

'No,' I cried to myself, as I shoved through another bunch of men blocking the way, almost punching at 'em. 'It can't be time, not yet. Jim, Birdy.'

My leg was almost totally cramped up, but there weren't no time for stamping it nor nothing. Just had to drag it along behind me. I even thought about dumping my kit, my gun and ammo an that, so I could go quicker. Especially the trenching tool bashing my leg. But I kept it all.

Then I realised the big guns was still going, ours as well as theirs. Not as much as before, or maybe I'd just got used to the sound, or the wind had changed or something. It didn't matter why, the barrage weren't over, that were the main thing. And men wasn't climbing up the ladders to go over the top. Not yet. They was all getting out their Tube Helmets and yanking 'em over their heads. It weren't the Big Push at all. It was the signal for gas, that's what the bells was. I almost laughed out loud.

Then I realised something else. As the men pulled on the gas masks, I couldn't see anybody's faces.

'Jim,' I starts shouting, as I hauled myself along. 'Jim, Birdy!'

But it were hopeless. My leg was almost giving up on me. I couldn't go much further. What if I'd already gone past 'em? Or taken a wrong turn somehow? There was other trenches linking up to this one, all over. And I knew it were stupid to be not putting on my gas mask an all. I dragged my leg along, grabbing men's shoulders an that to keep me upright. Exhausted from it all.

The trench were just packed too solid. I didn't think I could go another step.

24. OVER THE TOP

I pushed on slower than ever, knowing it were pointless. Everyone was in my way, and I was getting in their way an all, as men got themselves ready for the Push.

'Move along there, mate,' says a Kiltie coming up behind me. 'Officer coming through.'

I tried pressing myself against the side of the trench, but just ended up leaning against two blokes. One of them snapped at me, but there weren't nothing I could do. I ignored him.

'Tube Helmet, soldier,' the officer says, as he seed me. 'Come on lad. It's for your own good.'

I reached down and pulled the gas mask out, then looked up at the officer. Even though it were hard to hear that voice through the sound of the guns, and his thick canvas Tube Helmet, I knowed that accent.

'Noggin,' he says, letting me know I were right.

'What are you doing here?'

I stared into his mask. There, behind them stupid thick glass eye holes, was Edward Macpherson's little round glasses. Them eyes was so friendly looking, I could've cried out. Without waiting for me to answer his question, he grabbed my shoulder strap and set off again, taking me with him.

'Get that mask on, Noggin,' he shouts, as his soldier cleared a path for us. 'You're lucky the alarm bell is for our gas, not Fritz's. Hopefully it won't touch us. Come on.'

I weren't sure where I was being taked. I didn't care anymore, just hobbled along, tying the cords of the gas mask round my neck. I was with a friend, someone to care about me. Of course, Edward guessed what I were trying to do anyhow. Soon I seed more an more men who wasn't Kilties. They was Wiltshires, an I could see 'em clearer an clearer. The sun was rising proper. My stomach knotted up, a feeling of sick bubbling away down there. Soon it would be dawn, and it really would be time. In that light, I seed how hopeless it was to think I could find Jim an Birdy, even with Edward's help. There was just too many men, all looking the same in their groundsheet raincoats and sack gas masks. And there were dens like ours all along, everyone of 'em full to bursting.

In the end, it weren't me that did the finding. A hand grabbed out, and jerked me back against Edward's pulling.

'Oi,' shouts a voice I knowed well. 'Where the heck are you going, soldier?'

I ain't never been so glad to hear Adams' voice in all my life.

He pulled me in, back into the little den.

'There,' he says, shoving me at Jim an Birdy. 'He's back. No harm done. Happy now?'

The others pushed themselves towards me. Birdy first, then Jim an all, sticking one of them huge arms around me an pulling me close to him without a word, his other arm still clutching the football. I hugged back, an Birdy an all, shouting things about how glad I were to be back with 'em all. Even Adams.

'That's enough of that,' Adams shouts at me. 'I don't want you thinking you're gonna ruddy well kiss me.'

Them last couple of words ringed out through the trench. A few heads turned to look. Everything had gone quiet. At first I just thought the gas mask was making me deaf. But it weren't that. The mask made things a bit duller, but you could still hear alright through it. I stayed as still as I could, and strained my ears. There was no real noise of artillery no more. Just my own breathing and the far off enemy guns.

Our barrage was done now, for sure.

'Damn,' says Edward, looking at his wrist. 'It's time.'

Jim pulled me in a bit tighter, and I heared him speaking right next to me ear.

'Stamp that leg of yours, little brother,' he says through the mask. 'Time for us to give them Huns what for. Make Dad proud.'

Then his eyes flicked beyond me, an he holded his hand up an starting shaking it like he had a little bell. The foreman was speaking, and everybody had to listen. I turned and seed Adams there.

'You lot, stand to,' Adams shouts at us. 'Silence in the ranks.'

Edward Macpherson looked at me an Jim, an I swear I seed his eyebrows lifting.

'Thank you Corporal,' he says. 'You too.'

Adams did as he were told. I couldn't see them green eyes from where I was, but I bet they weren't happy. Edward was showing that he were an officer, not just a lad who'd left Glasgow University an stayed in our railway village on his way to war.

'Attention, men.' He shouts, and everyone turned to listen. Wiltshires as well as Camerons. 'In a few minutes we'll be going over. The artillery have been giving the Germans a good mashing, as you heard. Our objective is simple. We're to storm the trenches, and hold that position until reinforcements arrive. When we're in no-man's land, it's straight ahead keeping Lone Tree Ridge to our left and Tower Bridge to our right. You can't miss it. God bless, and give 'em Hell!'

Then he nodded at his Sergeant Major, and two orderlies gived out the rum ration. It were like syrup, thick an sweet. Not like the whisky Birdy gived us. But it made your belly feel warm, instead of sick. For a second anyway. As the man snatched the cup away from me, orders was shouted out, all down the line. With Adams doing his bit an all. We shuffled a bit forward, and got set so we was ready to go up the ladders. Only there weren't no proper ladders, just pegs banged into the muddy trench walls. Two Kilties was standing each side of our pegs, ready to lead us over the top. Edward was standing there between them. He rolled up his gas mask, put his whistle to his mouth an stared at his watch.

The final order was to fix bayonets. I stamped my foot like Jim said, and lifted my bayonet up to the barrel of my gun. I fumbled, but got it on just fine all the same. A hand come across, and slapped me on the shoulder. It were Birdy.

'Good lad,' he says to me. 'Let's show 'em what the Wiltshires can do with a Short Magazine Lee Enfield rifle. And slip your trenching tool round in front. It'll look after your crown jewels!'

I looked at him, but he were looking at Jim. I seed them nod at each other. Then I twigged what he meaned. I pulled the spade part of my trenching tool along my belt so it weren't by my side no more, but dangling in front. I was proper glad I hadn't dumped it.

Then we waited. There weren't much else to do. Some men was holding photos of their loved ones. Wives an kids an that. Some was saying prayers. I placed a hand over my tunic pocket and thinked about the letters in there. The one I wrote to Mam an Dad, in case anything should happen to me. And the one from Emma Deacon. Then I just standed there, listening to the rain on top of my mask, an the boom of German shells landing somewhere along our lines. And sometimes the crack of rifles shot by the Kilties on the firing step opposite us.

In front, all I could see was the backs of heads. Covered in them masks they barely looked like men at all, just sacks, piled up an waiting to be loaded on a train. And bayonets sticking up amongst 'em, catching the morning sun from above the trench top.

Then the rain stopped. Lieutenant Edward Macpherson blowed his whistle.

*

Every bone an muscle in my body tingled. Mostly

from being tired, I reckon, an hungry. And from being afraid. I thinked of Jim's five chances. When we was up on that parapet we'd be like sitting ducks. And the Hun would all just be there, guns ready, waiting for us to appear.

We shuffled forward and I seed the first Scottish soldiers clambering up them pegs an over the top of the pile of sandbags. Some of them came falling back straight away, and I knowed they was shot by the Hun. Edward led the other Kilties up, and then our men got their turn.

Jim and Birdy was in front of me, and I wanted to make sure I stayed with 'em. Adams was at the back, shouting at us an the rest of 2 Section to get a move on.

When we reached the pegs, Birdy yelled out.

'Come on lads. Let's bag us some Fritzies!'

My heart leaped, and I heared the sound of bagpipes.

I standed on the bottom peg, grabbed a higher one an pulled my way up, trying not to get kicked by Birdy's boots above me. My leg was still aching some, but not bad enough to stop me climbing. At the top, I pushed myself up off the sandbags 'til I was standing proper, and stamped again.

My breathing was going like a piston, blocking out every other sound inside that gas sack. I weren't able to take in what I was seeing through them eye glasses, not proper. All I could make out was black hills of coal spoil, and Tower Bridge looking close, and massive. Apart from that, it felt like I weren't in my own body. Like I was somewhere else, trying to watch but not able to understand. My chest was about to burst, my heart going so fast. To my left an my right, I half seed figures dropping to the ground in fits and jerks. Some of 'em clambered back up. Most stayed put, never to get up ever again.

In a rush, my body came back to me, an the scene cleared. The bagpipes was still playing, an I were still alive.

All over the show, explosions was rocking the earth, black bursts from the ground hammering my eardrums an throwing full grown men into the air. Between the booms, rifle fire an the death rattle of machine guns swept across the muddy ground, mowing down Wiltshires an Camerons without knowing or caring about the difference.

Putting one leg in front of the other, I stumbled forward with everyone else. All our training, all that time in Wiltshire and Basingstoke an at the Territorial Infantry Camp, was on ground that were sort of flat. This weren't like that at all. My bad leg could feel we was on a slope, with the enemy at the top firing down on us. That weren't all though. Every here an there, the earth rised up or dipped away. Shell holes and old trenches filled with water and bodies. In front of me, I seed some Kilties trying to climb over a smashed gun carriage tangled in barbed wire. A shrapnel bomb went off above 'em, bursting in a bluish-white puff with a hundred tiny flashes. In an instant, the men was turned into a soft, bloody bridge for the troops coming behind 'em.

The whole scene were filled with smoke an the shapes of other men going forward. Everything else were just grey and loud, with blasts of reds and oranges here an there. Shouting and guns, and screaming an all. I knowed what I had to do.

25. DEATH

We'd done Assault Training often enough. Just carry on walking forward at a normal rate, no matter what. We'd be up at the Hun trenches soon enough, then we could charge 'em. That's what we was there for. That was our job. I just thinked about the marching. Swinging that leg of mine as we worked our way up the sloping ground towards where Lone Tree Ridge must've been. Not that I knowed. Just followed the rest.

We was all carrying our Smellies to port, like we was told to, with the bayonet up an to the left. Everyone of us was the same. And with our masks on it weren't easy to know who was who. Except I were lucky. Jim's big shape were impossible to miss. He was holding his gun with one hand, and still had the football under his arm. Birdy standed out an all. Different to every other man there, he had his gun in the firing position, butt firmly into his shoulder. Aiming and just waiting to set eyes on a German. Ready to let 'em have it.

Another shell landed nearby us, then another. The bangs made my whole body reel an my teeth hurt. When I opened my eyes again, I was still standing but couldn't see nothing. I wiped at the glasses in my mask, but it didn't make much difference, on account of the smoke everywhere. I carried on stepping forward, and bumped into someone.

'Noggin,' the man shouts, and I thinked I hear Edward's accent. 'Keep on moving. We're on Lone Tree Ridge.'

He pointed, and I just about made out the shape of a battered tree in the smog. Then Edward put his face right in front of mine, so we could see each other better. We was both okay. Alive at least.

'Where's your brother?' He shouts.

There were another soldier there, with his back to us. I knowed from his size that it were Jim, and reached out an grabbed his shoulder.

'Jim,' I shouts. 'Jim.'

He turned round, and I seed my brother's eyes. But they was blank, like they didn't see me at all. Just staring down in front of him. I followed his look, and seed he were covered in mud, on his mask and all down his front and on his gun. But then I seed he weren't holding the ball no more. Instead, he had two guns, one in one hand and one in the other. He was staring at one of 'em. Then his head pulled up, and he shouted out.

'Birdy,' he says. 'Birdy.'

He pushed the gun at Edward, and that's when I knowed what it was. It were Birdy's gun. I'd recognise it anywhere. No other gun in the British army were polished that well, even though there was now mud on parts of it. And blood. But that weren't all. Gripping the butt of the gun there were a hand. Birdy's hand, and half his arm with his haversack hanging off it. His finger were still on the trigger.

My mind tried to work it out, but it couldn't. I looked round us. But there weren't no sign of any of the rest of him. Nothing.

'Oh God,' I said out loud, trying not to retch. 'Oh God. Birdy. Oh God.'

I felt my bad leg go weak, heat running up it. I reckon I would've felled back if it weren't for Edward being there to stop me. Then Adams was there, right in front of me and shouting. Even through his mask, I could see his green eyes screwed up with more anger than I ever seed before.

'Get on you dirty slouchers,' he shouts at us, his voice almost shaking. 'Shirkers'll be shot. Get a move on!'

I seed him flick his eyes at Edward, then turn away and stomp off in the direction of the German trenches. Edward didn't say nothing. He knowed Adams was right, an I knowed it an all. Without a word, Edward snatched the gun off Jim and chucked it to one side. With Birdy's hand. Then he set himself in front of me and Jim an speaked to us.

'There's nothing to be done,' he says, shaking his head. 'Come on.'

Jim just standed there, looking at his own empty hand. It were shining red, all over his fingers. Birdy's blood. Edward pushed Birdy's bag into the hand, so Jim had something else to think about.

'Can't imagine your friend would want to see his rations go to waste,' Edward says. 'Now, come on, let's get moving again. Follow me.'

Only Jim had something else on his mind. As Edward got moving I did as he telled us, an followed. But my brother weren't next to me. I turned round and seed him strapping Birdy's bag over his shoulder and staring down at the ball.

'Come on, Jim,' I shouts out.

Slowly, I seed his head lift up. Then he pulled back his foot, screamed at the top of his voice and kicked that football harder than he'd ever kicked anything. I ducked, couldn't help it, thinking the thing was coming my way. But it went beyond me, and were quickly followed by my brother. Still roaring through that gas mask, he charged past me, swinging his rifle in front of him. I gasped for breath. My brother. What was he doing? As he ran past Edward, I wanted to shout out, but no words comed. Then something happened what I weren't ready for.

Jim ran past Adams but instead of shouting at Jim, Adams joined him running, an he shouted an all. Then I heared a cheering, an when I looked, all the men behind, left an right of us, the rest of our company, was all taking off an all. As fast as their legs would carry 'em, jumping over barbed wire and the bodies of their mates, and following their footie star.

Edward an me was standing there, watching. Reckon he was as dumbfounded as I were. But he soon got himself together, yanking out his revolver and joining in the rush, shouting as loud as the rest of 'em. I didn't give it another thought. My mouth opened and I yelled an all. And followed my brother. My heart was racing and so was my mind. In between each gasp for air, I could picture that hand. Birdy. I don't even know if he even got to fire that blessed gun of his. But I knowed there weren't no use in thinking like that, an tried not to, turning my mind to keeping up with them others, an Jim. It weren't easy. My leg saw to that.

More men fell down in front of me. Some just sort

of slumped, soft like. Others looked like they was hit by a steam train. I seed men being just lifted off the ground an flipped into the air. All from the non-stop shooting of that invisible enemy up ahead of us.

I tried to figure out where folk was. Jim had vanished with the crowd, all going faster than I were able to stay with. And there seemed to be a load of Kilties there an all, making it impossible to know where Edward was. My eyes flicked from one shapeless figure to the next. Just hundreds of men, all the same. I swear could hear my heart beating in between the breaths inside that mask. It were going so fast.

'Jim,' I tried shouting, though my voice was just a croak. 'Jim Arkell. Where are you?'
I tried to slow my breathing some. It were getting even harder to see through them glass eyeholes, what with me puffing an blowing inside that sack. Soon, I couldn't see nothing, an all I could think to do was untie the cords an stick my hand up inside to wipe the glass. We was told not to do that, but I knowed it were the only way to clean them things. As soon as that air rushed in though, my stomach turned with the stench.

I was still going uphill a bit, across a field. Only whatever crop was there once, was now trod into it and mud, an the place were covered in shell holes and rolls of barbed wire, and bodies. Too many dead an wounded to count. I could see it all again with my clear eye glasses. But the taste of the air was bitter and burning, and smelled like things I didn't want to think about. It rasped at the back of my throat and made my belly feel like I were going to heave. My mouth were dry, no spit. Not even enough to clean the glass.

Quick as I could, I pulled the cords in, stuffing the edges of the mask down inside my collar. I set off again, just hoping I ain't been gassed. I needed to find Jim, or Edward Macpherson, or anyone else what I knowed. Any moment I were sure that poison gas was going to burn out my insides and I were going to fall down dead. Jim and Edward, and Adams an that, would just go on without me. And when they seed I weren't with 'em no more, they'd just shrug an carry on. Nothing more to be done. That was just how it was.

But I didn't fall down. The taste didn't go away, but I didn't throw up. Maybe it weren't gas I was tasting, just smoke, and sulphur an lime. And death.

There weren't time to dwell on it, mind. Another man got hit by a bullet, right near me. Dropped to his knees then sank forward, his masked face into the mud. I trotted on by.

Somehow, the sound of bullets was all I could hear

after that. Whistling as they flied by. It were a short, sweet sort of sound that were gone before you knowed it had arrived. Up ahead of me, the clouds of smoke drifted and puffed away, blue, brown, pink, yellow, like a load of locomotives was dancing somewhere below, their stacks bellowing out smog just to create a show for me.

It took a new sound to bring me back to realness. A machine gun, crackling an tapping away from one of them black spoil hills. It weren't just the sound. In the smoke across my view, men was dropping. Left, right an centre. The football team was torn to shreds. They weren't going to make it to the opposition's goal line. My first thoughts went to Jim of course. He was leading that crowd. And with his size he had to be about the easiest target the Hun had ever had. I runs forward, using every muscle in my body to keep my bad leg going. Just praying it wouldn't seize up, and grabbing at barbed-wire screw posts an that for extra support.

I didn't get far though, before a man lying in my path waved me down. I was thinking he was wounded, but I didn't have no time to stop. Had to carry on. Ignore him. It were only as I got closer that I heared he were shouting my name.

26. CAPTURE

'Get down, Arkell,' the man yells. 'You ruddy idiot. Get down now, Private, or I'll have you shot.'

Adams. He was lying on the edge of a crater, him an maybe a dozen others. They all had their gas masks rolled up like hats. Seeing 'em down there made me feel naked somehow. Exposed. I throwed myself down, almost knocking the wind out of my chest.

'Get here,' Adams says, yanking me next to another familiar shape. 'You can undo your tube helmet. There's no gas here. And stay still, that machine gun's giving Hell.'

'Jim,' I says to the bloke lying next to me, rolling my mask up. 'Jim. Is that you?'

Jim turned his head, an we stared at each.

'Noggin,' he says to me, with a tiny nod of his head.

My heart could've sung out. My brother was alright, and I'd found him. I lay my head back, and let out a long slow breath.

'Noggin,' Jim says again. 'Birdy.'

I turned my face round to look at him again. But before I could say a thing, another voice spoke. Edward Macpherson was there an all.

'Okay lads,' he says. 'We're going to take it out. I'll lead. Who's got wire-cutters.'

Adams said he had some. Before I hardly had a chance to catch my breath, him and Edward was off again. Down into the crater, then up the other side and crawling out onto the field again, the spoil heap looming over us. A black mountain blocking out the light. Me an Jim an the rest just had to follow. The machine gun got louder an louder. We was getting closer to it. Then I seed what it were doing.

Away to our left, the next wave was coming. Smellies to port, hundreds of figures striding forward like ghosts. Only they was being shot down. Not one at a time. Whole rows of 'em. Walking one minute, piled up in the dirt the next. They was all heading straight at where that machine gun was, buried away somewhere in the coal spoil behind yards of barbed wire an that. The Huns just had to sit there and feed it bullets. More targets kept pouring in, taking the place of them what had already fallen. Adams had saved me from the same thing.

I scraped along on my belly, doing all I could not to look up any more. Before we got far, we seed the barbed wire defences. Like a forest of curling steel brambles, spikes all over. Our barrage was supposed to have blown that all to bits. But it clear hadn't. Not here anyhow. We didn't hang about though, 'cause we knowed we must be real close. We lay down even flatter, an Adams produced a pair of wire-cutters and started clipping away.

'Gas!' Edward shouts out.

In an instant we was all pulling our masks down again, and tying them tight round our necks. One of our lads weren't so lucky, mind. A low, sick green cloud rolled in around us, an I seed he didn't have no mask. Must've taken it off altogether, or lost it somehow. His face turned scared straight off, and he clutched at his throat. He turned to us, to Edward, hoping for help. But there weren't nothing we could do and in a second he was retching, as the gas burnt his insides. His screams turned to raw, rasping gasps for air, and he tried to clamber to his feet. All I could do was watch them white eyes flicking all over the place, blood gurgling up from his scorched lungs.

We lost some more lads after that. Hit by bullets and gone. Soon there was just me and Jim, and Edward an Adams. We pushed on. Cutting, crawling an cutting some more.

Our first German trench weren't much of one. It were more of a scraping in the ground, a cutting, along the edge of the coal spoil. I could see chunks of it was all collapsed in, with piles of mud an black dust. Probably thanks to our big guns. We rolled down and lay in the bottom. We was safer there than up on that field.

'This way,' shouts Edward, leads us along the cutting. 'This should get us closer to that machine gun.'

We worked our way along for what felt like hours but were probably only minutes, expecting Huns to appear at every corner. The sound of the machine gun got real loud, even though we couldn't see it none. Edward kept bobbing his head up above the trench, an so did Adams. I tried to keep mine down, and told Jim to do the same. But it weren't easy for him.

As we came round a corner, we was looking down a long stretch of empty ditch. Adams dropped down in the mud, looking at us an pointing away to his right.

'Got it,' he spits out under his breath. 'It's right there. That way.'

'Are you sure?' Whispers Edward, as we all squat down and close up together.

'I seen their stupid spikey helmets,' says Adams, fumbling with his webbing. 'Looks like they've set up a nest in the slag heap itself.'

Edward holded a hand up.

'Sssh,' he says, his eyes widening inside his sack.

We all listened hard. German voices. Even with the noises of shells an rifle fire an that, I could hear 'em, couldn't be hardly any distance from us. Maybe round the very next corner. Adams pulled some things out of his bag. Two Mill's bombs. Grenades. One of the five pound bombs in each hand. He looked to Edward, then turned and scurried further along the trench, quiet as he were able. At the end of the stretch he stopped and sat against the wall, looking back at us. He shaked his head, putting down one of the Mills and stabbing a finger here an there up above him.

'Damn,' whispers Edward. 'He can't tell where the gun nest is from there. He doesn't know which direction to throw the bombs.'

I knowed straight away what to do. I swinged round to Jim and looked him in the eye. He stared back at me through his mask, a deep sad stare. If we was to sort this, I needed his help. But I couldn't tell if he would go along with it. I didn't say a word. Instead, I first held up my hand, in Emma's stripy glove, and made like it were talking. One of Dad's signals. Sign language. Jim responded straight away and I let out a deep breath inside my gas helmet. For just a second it were like we was back home, making signs at each other behind Dad so he couldn't see us. We both made a few signs, then shaked hands an nodded. We had a plan. Edward didn't understand what we was up to, of course, and grabbed at me as I turned to go off down the trench towards Adams. I gived him the thumbs up. A sign even he would get. He let me go.

When I reached Adams, I seed his green eyes flashing inside his mask, an his eyebrows raising. He didn't get what we was doing neither. But I paid no heed, just lay back against the wall, same as him, and held my Smelly in front of me like I was presenting arms to an officer. Then I watched Jim. He'd moved right back. He ripped off his gas mask and rubbed coal dust over his face, so it were better blended with the wall of the ditch. For a moment, it made me remember back to the coal heap we had to move, an how angry that made Adams. I turned to look. Adams was looking at Jim, but when he looked back at me, one of them green eyes of his winked. I turned back to watch Jim, an couldn't help half smiling to myself.

Jim hadn't keeled over, so I knowed there was no gas. Even so, I thinked of that poor bloke, and decided not to rip my mask off proper. Just roll it up so I could see better.

Ever so slow, Jim raised himself up to full height, so his head were just above the parapet. He pointed two fingers towards his eyes and then towards me. He could see the machine gunners. He put one hand out in front of him, and turned it like a hand on a clock. Dead slow. I copied with the rifle, like in a mirror. Next to me, I seed Adam's head moving, nodding. He got it, and moved away a couple of paces, watching me an preparing the first of the bombs.

Jim's hand stopped. So did mine. Then my brother held both hands in front of his chest, and pumped 'em towards me. The foreman's signal to the rivet gun team. Everyone was in place. Everything was set. Go.

It seemed funny to use that signal, looking like Jim were using a machine gun. I nodded to Adams. His green eyes twinkled inside his mask. He lobbed the first bomb up over the trench wall, in the direction my bayonet was telling him. Then the other one. We both ducked down and covered our heads. The booms didn't seem so loud when they came. We both got covered in black dust an that, but the sound was dull and distant. We shaked our heads, and I listened again. There weren't no machine gun noise no more. Maybe we'd done it. But Adams didn't plan on celebrating any.

'Come on,' he says. 'We need to make sure.'

We looked back at Edward. Him an Jim scampered towards us, an we all ran to where the bombs had done their work. After squeezing down a tiny joining-trench, we climbed into that nest, a hollow dug into the edge of the spoil heap and protected by a wall of sandbags an more of the black stuff. There I seed my first Huns. Hard to say how many, chucked about the place, legs an arms sticking out. Four or five of 'em maybe. All dead. In the middle of 'em, their dull grey, heavy machine gun was sitting there on its tripod sledge, like it didn't have a care in the world.

'We need to knobble it, Lieutenant,' says Adams, slapping the gun. 'Make sure them beggers can't get it going again. Anyone else got any Mills? That was my lot.'

None of us did. We sat there for a moment, then Edward speaked.

'We can't stay,' he says. 'The Hun'll be here any time. We'll just have to topple it over or something. Best we can do.'

But as I stared at that gun, I seed brown liquid dripping from the metal casing round its barrel. My mind were still going ten to the dozen after the sign language plan had worked. Another picture popped into my head. What Jim said about that motor cycle.

Even an idiot knows you can't run a machine without oil.

'What about its oil, Jim?' I says, all excited and pointing. 'Can't we empty its oil?'

'Don't be daft,' he mutters, with a slight shake of his head. 'Why would they want oil in the barrel. With the number of bullets that thing fires per second, it gets bloomin' hot. That's the cooling system. Dirty water.'

I slumped, and turned back to Edward. Shrugging my shoulders. But Edward straightened up, and clicked open the cylinder on his revolver, popping out the spent cartridges an loading in fresh ones. Then he snapped it shut again.

'That'll do,' he says. 'Nice one lads. A few punctures should delay things a bit at least. Move back.'

We all moved away, an Edward let rip with his Webley, shooting two or three holes in the metal surrounding the gun's barrel. Adams pointed out that there were two spare barrels laid there on the ground. They got the same treatment.

I don't know if the pistol fire telled the Germans we was there, but next thing we knowed, there was shouting and noises along the trench. We clambered out of the machine gun nest. But we was too late. Bullets flied everywhere, an all we could do was throw ourselves down on the ground, part protected by the nest's sandbags. I tried to pull my Smelly round, like we was trained to do, but the strap was caught under me, tangled in with my ammo pouches. My trenching tool was pressing into me too. I feeled panic rising up in my guts.

'No, no, no, no,' I says to myself, tearing at the gun strap. 'I ain't gonna die. Not now. Mam.'

Then above the shouting in German and the gunshots, a crystal clear voice rang out.

'Don't shoot,' Adams shouted at the top of his voice. 'We surrender. Don't shoot!'

'What are you doing, Adams?' Shouted Edward. 'We're doing no such thing. Get back here this instant.'

I twisted around, an the strap finally got free. Adams was standing up. He throwed down his Smelly and stuck his hands in the air, using his wiry body to block off the joining-trench so the Hun weren't able to see us.

'Not you, sir,' he says, without looking back. 'You and the rest of the lads scarper, I'll keep 'em busy.'

27. INJURY

We shuffled across the chalky mud an coal dust, and somehow found ourselves rolling back into the broken down trench. Me, Jim and Edward Macpherson. Jim were in front. He shouts an I seed him pull his gun up to his shoulder, and fire. The noise made me jolt, and I pulled my gun up and shoots an all, without even thinking about it. And so did Edward, with his pistol. Jim shoots again, two times, then draws back and waves us down.

Then I could see what we'd been shooting at. Something moving. Huns. My first sight of real live ones. Rushing along and ducking down into spaces an behind piles of dirt of the crashed in trench.

I was holding my gun right in front o' me, all ready to fire again. My finger was on the trigger and I was watching the Hun down the barrel. I didn't shoot, just stared. But they didn't wait. The first one fired and it all kicked off. The trench was alive with the noise of their guns and with bullets singing in my ears and thudding into the earth around me. Jim started firing back and I gets a grip at last, an fired that Smelly like there weren't no tomorrow.

If I hit anyone or not, I'll never know. Just kept pulling that trigger 'til there weren't no bullets left. The others must've run out an all, and the Fritzies, come to that. It went quiet just as quick as it had gone noisy in the first place. Everybody was reloading, them and us.

'We've got to get out of here,' shouts Edward, shoving bullets into his cylinder. 'There're too many of them.'

Then the firing started up again. And it weren't just from where the Hun was before.

'Above,' shouts Jim, swinging round and letting off several rounds.

I twisted to see where he were pointing. On the trench top, was the heads of more Huns, ducking up and down. I didn't see no faces mind. Under their dirt coloured spiked helmets, each of 'em was hidden behind a gas mask. They looked like devils to me. I don't know what we looked like to them.

Pulling my gun to my shoulder I looked down the sights best I could. One of them Huns rised up, right there in my view. He was that close I seed the look of surprise in his eyes as he spots me. If he went to shoot, he were too late. I pulled the trigger and felt the recoil bash my shoulder where I weren't holding the gun proper. That Hun slumped forward and I knowed he was dead for sure. But another one appeared in his place. I did the same again. They kept on coming.

'Come on Noggin,' Jim shouted. 'We have to go over the top. Get back on the field.'

We backed away. Edward keeped on shooting 'til he ran out of bullets again. But the Hun didn't leave us be. Them on the top leaped down into the trench. The first one were sorry about that straight away, I reckon. He threw himself onto Jim's bayonet. The noise were like a butcher's cleaver bedding into a side of pork.

I downed two more, but Edward were still reloading an was just about to get a Fritz bayonet through him. That was when I thinked of that football, and Cock Canary's so-called bayonet training. My lungs let out the biggest scream of their lives, and I ran at that Hun fast as I were able.

I saw my bayonet blade going into him, through his arm and on clear through his chest, right up to its hilt. Then I pulled the trigger and fired. I didn't mean to, it just sort of happened. The bullet throwed the man off the blade. He collapsed away, and left me there with his blood dripping off the bayonet. Jim finished off his Hun and we both looked up. There was more of 'em coming along the trench, firing at us.

Before I could think anymore about it, I feeled Jim's huge hands on me. Then up I went, onto the top of the trench. Two seconds after, Edward was throwed up next to me, and we both turned and helped Jim up an all.

Keeping low, we ran, back through the gaps Adams had made in the barbed wire earlier.

I could still hear bullets flying, and I weren't about to slow down. I scampered along, half bent over, half upright. Soon, I seed the end of the wire defences and followed Jim an Edward back on to the field. But I only got about two yards when the whole place blowed up in front of me.

There was nothing. Nothing to hear, nothing to see. I were just lying there, feeling like I was floating on a cloud, an everything was black.

'Noggin,' I hears, after a time that could've been a second, could've been ten years for all I knowed. 'Noggin. Is that you? You alright mate?'

I pushed up onto my elbows, and feeled the earth beneath me. A bullet whistles by, then another.

'I ain't dead then? I asks.

'No, you ain't dead, you daft monkey. Now get down.'

214

It were Jim.

'Am I blind, Jimmy,' I asks, all matter of fact, as I let myself lay back again.

He didn't answer. Instead, I felt a tugging, then my gas mask were teared off, causing it's rough canvas to scratch over my face. It must've slipped down over my face, the eyeholes covered in mud. Without it, the world were bright and clear. And there was Jim, his eyebrows all scrunched and looking down at me.

'You been hit at all?' he asks.

I pulled my head up so I can look down at the rest of me, and felt about, making sure I was all there. Jim didn't wait for an answer.

'We're going to find the Lieutenant,' he says. 'When I say go, you have to come with me. Okay?'

'Oh,' I said, blinking my eyes, and twisting my head over so I could see him.

He were lying flat on his back, same as me, staring straight up and holding his rifle against his chest with both hands. Men was running past us and I could still hear shooting going on. Jim took two deep breaths, then rolled over and up onto his haunches.

'Go,' he shouts.

My gun! Where was my gun? I felt about me, my hands going as quick as they could. Found it, right there along by me. At least I reckoned it were my gun, not someone else's. It didn't matter much. Then I done the same as Jim, an rolled over to make it easier to get on my knees.

I turned round to find where he'd gone, and seed him throw himself forward and disappear. I didn't wait. Just jumped up and ran some, an throwed myself after him.

Mud and water splashed all over my face. It were cold. I snatched a breath, and pulled myself up so my face weren't right in it. We was in a big hole what a shell must've made. It had shallow muddy sides and a pool of water across its bottom. There was other soldiers laid there, piled on top of each other and not moving any. It were hard to say which bit belonged to which body. Jim was crawling round to the other side of the crater, and shouting.

'Edward,' he shouted. 'Edward Macpherson.'

In a second, he stopped crawling and starts digging. Only he didn't bother with his trenching spade, just burrowed into the mud with both his huge hands, flicking it all over the shop. I moved towards him, an then I seed something.

Where he was digging, a hand appeared. At first, I didn't understand, and just carried on towards him. Then there was a rushing feeling inside, spreading from my guts an right through me.

'Edward,' I shouted, same as Jim, grabbing at the

216

hand and pulling. 'Edward.'

I couldn't see anything except an arm, standing up there in the mud, all alone. Like some horrible plant. I didn't know if it were dead or alive. Then Jim's digging cleared a shoulder, then a gas mask, which he teared off. There was Edward, stock still and smeared in dirt. I joined in the digging and soon Jim were able to get a grip on Edward's tunic collars, and yanked with all his might. Edward's head came up from the dirt, and Jim shaked him, all the while shouting. We was both shouting.

'Edward,' we says.

I grabbed Edward's hand again, and squeezed hard. After a second or two I felt it moving. I clutched it tight, and the moving got stronger. Soon, he were gripping me back as hard as I were holding him. Then he spluttered, and two white wide eyes appeared in the dirty face, his glasses was hanging off one ear. I put them back over his nose.

'Noggin, ' I heared him say, ever so faint. 'Jim.'

'You're alright now, chum,' says Jim. 'It's okay. We's here.'

Then Jim starts digging away more of the mud. I pulled myself up a bit, so my face is nearer Edward's, still clutching his hand.

'Noggin,' he says to me, and I think there's a bit of a smile on his face. 'You alright lad?'

I told him I were fine. Then Jim stopped digging, and looked up at me.

'Will you be able to get my legs clear any time soon?' Edward says. 'They're really aching.'

I looked down. Jim had cleared away the mud from Edward's legs. Only there weren't no legs there.

Edward's tunic were still in good order. Beyond it, there was his kilt. But where the knees was, that was where his legs stopped. I shuffled down so I were closer to where Jim was. I had my hand over my mouth, an could taste the dirt. Jim were just kneeling there, staring at the place where Edward's legs should've been. I tried to push him out of the way, and dug with my hands. They had to be there somewhere. Maybe they was just bent under him.

The mud was thick and full of chalk and water an coal dust. I had to cup it away with both hands. I digged and digged, throwing the sludge aside and saying to myself they has to be here. They has to be. My eyes was stinging, an I could feel my lips shaking. The more mud I cleared away, the more I saw how things really was.

Edward's legs was ripped off just under the knees. His kilt was perfect. But there was nothing beyond it except two jagged stumps, caked with mud and blood. No sign of his boots, or his feet. The mud were coming away red in my hands.

28. MADNESS

'Just leave it,' Jim says, pulling me away. 'It's no good. Leave it.'

But I fought against him, trying to elbow him out of my way. He were stronger an me though, of course, and pulled me to him and puts his arms around me, and I just buried my head into his shoulder and cried, bashing my fist against his chest.

'Noggin,' I hears Edward saying. 'Noggin. What's the matter? You alright?'

'Of course,' I answer, wiping my eyes an turning back so he can see my face. 'I'm just fine, Edward. No need to worry about me.'

'You see what I mean?' Edward says, staring past me. 'Just about to drop something else. Wrong time of year.'

I didn't have a clue what he was going on about.

He was losing it. Talking nonsense. Did that mean he was going to die? I had to fight back the tears.

'You'll be fine,' I says, trying not to show the fear in my voice. 'We's going to get you back to the Medics. They'll patch you up good and proper. You'll be back in Blighty before you knows it. Back at Glasgow University.'

'Look,' he says, and lifts his hand to point up.

I turned, not expecting to see anything. But there, hanging above us over the edge of the crater was the branches of a tree. Black and knobbly, like burnt limbs, with long red leaves hanging off here an there, as if they was drops of blood, waiting to fall. My mouth fell open, and I heared myself gasp. It was a wild cherry tree. We was on Lone Tree Ridge, and the tree was just the same as mine back in the cemetery at home.

Except of course it weren't just the same. Most of it was blown away, and the bits left behind had so many bullet holes through 'em they was like Mam's vegetable colanders. And the dead men all around it was on top of the ground instead of under it.

I dropped back an lay still, next to Edward. Everything seemed very quiet.

'I'll see you there again one day, maybe,' he says. 'At your cherry tree. Shame about you two not being apprentices together, though. You would've made a good team, I'd say.'

Then he looked at me.

'What did you mean about the Medics?'

I stuttered. Before I got the words sorted, Edward pulled up his head, straining his neck to look down his body. At where his legs was supposed to be.

'Oh God,' he says.

His head fell back, and he stared up into the sky, past the cherry tree leaves.

'Oh God. Oh God, ' he repeated to himself, over and over.

I didn't know what to do. My guts knotted right through, then I swinged round and throwed up.

Edward didn't say nothing else, just moaned. A long, low moan that made the nerves up my spine tingle. I turned to Jim. He was kneeling there, staring. As he seed me looking at him, he turned away and looked into his haversack. Only he didn't have just one bag, of course. He had Birdy's as well as own, and he pulled out a whisky bottle. Except there weren't much bottle left. Just a broken jagged neck.

'Aha,' says Jim, chucking the bottle aside an fumbling in the bag again. 'Time for a fag, I think.'

He pulled out Birdy's baccy tin, smeared the mud off his hands best he were able, and maked something like a cigarette. It took him three goes.

'Jim,' I says. 'Come on, what are you doing? We

needs to get Edward back.'

'It ain't a pretty smoke,' is all he says back, without looking at me, an getting out Birdy's matches. 'But as long as it fires up, I'll be happy.'

The matches was dry. Jim lit the fag and offered it to Edward who says yes, which were a bit of a surprise to me 'cause he ain't never smoked before. Jim held the fag to Edward's lips and Edward took a draw, then coughed, spitting up blood.

'It ain't so good from here in, Lieutenant Edward. If I'm honest,' says Jim, taking a puff on the bloody cigarette himself. 'Minute we stick our head up there, reckon there's a few Fritzies waiting to take a pot shot at us.'

Then his eyes glazed over.

'What the heck was Adams up to?' He says, shaking his head. 'Giant sausages and German beer? That what he was after? Bloomin' idiot!'

Then he laughed. My belly wound up. I swinged round and whacked his arm with the back of my hand.

'Jim!' I says. 'What're you on about? He did it for us. Leave it be. What about Edward? What're we going to do about Edward?'

Jim just carried on laughing. I had to hit him again. Harder this time. Real slowly, he turned and looked at me. Then he slapped me on the back.

'Good thinking, Noggin,' he says, sticking the fag in his mouth. 'Come on, let's get old Eddie back to the Medics.'

I didn't like the way he was talking. I liked it better when he was quiet an sulky. Or angry even, wild. But then he shifted himself round so he could get hold under Edward's armpit, so I figured maybe it was going to be alright. I done the same on my side, and we tried to tug Edward out of the mud.

It weren't easy. The mud held on, clinging to what was left of Edward's body. We pulled and yanked, and I tried to dig away some of the sludge as Jim used his extra strength to move Edward. As we moved up the crater wall, I kept slipping back, and the harder Jim pulled, the more his own legs slided into the mud, an the more Edward moaned.

When we was near the top, Jim flopped down next to Edward and I pulled myself next to 'em. I didn't know what to do next. I reckoned that as soon as we was out of the shell crater we would be easy picking for them Huns. But we couldn't just sit there with Edward in that state. And he were getting worse an all. The moaning stopped, and I seed that he were out cold. We had to go on, and I told Jim that.

'Yes, Noggin,' he snaps at me. 'Don't I flippin' well know it.'

Then he stared at me, pulling the fag butt off his

lip.

'What did he mean,' he says. 'About us not being apprentices together?'

'Eh?' Was all I thought to say. 'What are you on about now Jim? Come on. Please. We have to get him back, or he'll die.'

'They all know, don't they?' Jim muttered, turning away from me. 'Everyone knows what an idiot I am.'

My mind was a blur, and I shaked my head, getting cross with my brother. I knowed what he was thinking. That maybe Edward reckoned he couldn't be an apprentice after what he'd done with the bike. Stupid. Edward were talking about me not wanting to be an apprentice. He weren't saying nothing about Jim. I opened my mouth, wanting to tell Jim so. But he grabbed hold of Edward again and pulled. I crawled alongside.

In a few moments we was out of the crater, back on the field. But it weren't how I expected at all. For one thing, it were much quieter. Well, quieter in one way anyhow. There weren't hardly any shooting going on. Just the odd rifle firing, but no rattling machine guns. Even the Hun's big guns seemed to have quietened down, though there was still some shells falling. The main noise I could hear was the crying out.

'Bloody Hell,' says Jim, looking around him.

I slowly raised up a bit, to see what he were looking at. First I looked toward the Hun lines. I could just make out where the trenches was, beyond the barbed wire. But what caught my eye, and make me look about, was the men. The field were covered with bodies. Our lads. Everywhere I looked, there was just men lying there, like they was all just kipping down together, the way we did plenty of times in training. Most of 'em wasn't moving none, and the way they was laid, twisted, telled you straight off that they weren't just asleep.

I ducked back down again, and took some deep breaths. I thought of Edward's wounds, and of him being one of them bodies.

'Come on, Jim,' I says. 'We need to keep going.'

Jim looked at me, then let go of Edward. His great hands was shaking. He got up, real slow.

'Jim,' I says. 'Jim, please. Please! What are you doing? Get down! Please.'

But he wouldn't listen. He stood up straight, and looked round him, first one way, then the other. Then he unbuckled his webbing an that, let it all drop, and walked away.

29. SURVIVAL

I lay down next to Edward, and closed my eyes.

My teeth was clamped together, an there were stinging behind my eyes. But there weren't no time for feeling sorry for myself. Nor Jim neither. I had to help Edward. That were all I could think. Had to.

Shifting myself a bit, I managed to get so I were lying higher up than Edward with my legs each side of his shoulders. I shoved my hands under his armpits and took in some breaths, and pulled. All I could manage was to tug him forward a foot or so, then shuffle myself back and do it again. He were heavier than I could've imagined, but at least we was moving. I just had to pull hard, that was all, even if I kept slipping, or losing my grip. Just had to hope them Huns didn't pick me off.

Some of the men we had to get past didn't look like men no more. Just things, mixed with mud and blood and bones and army issue cloth. Some of them cried out as we went by, or over them. But there weren't nothing I could do. I already had Edward. Couldn't help any others.

'Don't worry, mate,' I says to 'em, in between breaths. 'Medics'll be here soon.'

I did see some stretcher bearers an all, and other men helping out. The shooting seemed to have stopped altogether. The medics was all just walking about, almost normal like. But there weren't enough of 'em. And when I shouted, it were useless. They was too busy.

'Fritz is giving us a ceasefire to get the wounded back,' one of them shouts to me. 'Get your mate back quick as you can, son. It won't last long.'

Hearing that an seeing them medics standing up, carrying stretchers, or pushing 'em on wheels, made me feel I was able to get up a bit an all and drag Edward that bit quicker. Somehow, my bad leg weren't a problem neither. I feeled a bit of that heat going up it, but it never stiffened up none. Even so, the whole time I were expecting the firing to start up again and a bullet to come by especially for me. But it didn't.

At last, I seed the row of sandbags which I knowed was ours. I almost cheered, my arms was hurting that much with the tugging.

Before we reached the trench, a voice shouts out. It sounded Scottish.

'Oi, you,' it said. 'This ceasefire ain't gonna last. This way, quick.'

Squinting, I just about made out the tartan on a side cap. A Cameron, waving at me. Then I twigged what he meaned. I could hear shooting again. All over I seed them stretcher bearers running back as fast as they could. I shouted out, and tugged all in a panic like, to get Edward to the trench.

I chucked myself onto the parapet sandbags, and the Cameron soldier was there to help, pulling his officer's body across sideways. Me an Edward both rolled over the top. Before I knowed what was happening, someone grabbed at my arm and I was dragged off the bags. Then I felt myself falling, and landing in the mud with a splash. My arms buckled under me but I paid no heed, just rolled over to see what was happening.

'Edward,' I yelled, as I looked about me.

Four or five Jocks was there, at the wall of the trench, pulling Edward off the parapet. His injuries was all too clear. Someone helped me up. Along with the Kilties there was two other men, an they was holding on to Edward. I pushed my way in amongst 'em all.

'What're you doing?' I asks, trying to grab Edward.

'Leave him be. He's got to get down the Line. To the dressing station, or field hospital.'

'It's okay, mate,' says one of the men, pointing at his arm. 'We'll take good care of him, don't you fret none.'

I looked at the man's sleeve. It had a dirty white band wrapped around it, with a red cross. Then I looked in his face. He smiled, and turned back to Edward. I wiped the mud from my face, and watched as they laid Edward down on a stretcher. Then they lifted it up. I stood by and held Edward's hand, an he gripped me back.

'Noggin,' he says, though it was only a whisper and he don't open his eyes none.

'Edward,' I says back, and clutches both my hands round his. 'Edward. It's alright. I'm here. You're alright now. Medics'll look after you now.'

'See you under the tree,' he mutters.

Then the Medic told me they had to get going, for Edward's sake. And I had to let go.

'He's going to be alright,' I says. 'Ain't he?'

'Don't you worry, mate,' one of them Medics says, raising his eyebrows some. 'I'm sure he'll be well enough to see you get a ruddy medal.'

*

Two Scotsmen got me an ammo box to sit on. They said some things to me, friendly like, but I couldn't really hear 'em.

I don't know how long I sat there, just staring at the mud in front of me. Pictures of Birdy and Adams and Edward Macpherson flitted round my head, and Jim. Where was Jim? Where was my brother? Maybe one hour passed, maybe more. I sort of knowed I should've been doing something, or feeling something at least. But there weren't nothing in me. All I could do was stare.

The trench weren't anything like as busy as it had been early that day. One of the Jocks gave me a brew, and I thanked him.

Then someone shouted from the firing step, a bit further down the trench. I didn't take no notice at first, until there was more shouting an that. Some of the Jocks crowded round where their mate had called out. I got up and walked slowly along, with the tea.

'What is it?' I asked, when I got to 'em, hardly daring to hope.

But they didn't need to answer.

A figure appeared, standing as tall as you like on the parapet. He had his arms stretched to the Heavens, and was shouting at the top of his voice. Jim. I dropped the mug of tea. My mouth wanted to shout out, but my voice clammed up on me. All the Jocks was shouting at him anyhow, telling him not to be so stupid and to get down. Whether he was listening to 'em or not, I couldn't tell. But he vanished, turning away from the trench.

'Oh God, Jim,' I says to myself, running to where he'd gone and clambering up the pegs. 'Jim, what're you doing?'

I took a breath, then pushed my eyes up above the parapet. My heart was going ten to the dozen, fully expecting to see my brother laid there, dead. In fact, I couldn't see him at all, but I could hear him, chattering away at the top of his voice. With another deep breath, I crawled out onto the field, and inched my way forward. Rifles was going off, from our side an theirs, and somewhere in the back of my head it sounded like their artillery was starting to get going an all.

I loosened my webbing so I could move easier and be less of a target, and slid over the edge of a shell crater. There was Jim, scrabbling about on his knees.

'Must be here,' he were saying, over an over. 'Must keep on.'

'Jim,' I says, scrambling down to him and grabbing at his sleeve. 'Jim. What're you doing? We has to get back. Come on.'

Jim looked me, right in the eye. But my brother didn't seem to know me.

'Can't stop,' he says, pulling his arm away. 'Got to keep looking.'

'Jim,' I shouts, feeling like my chest were going to burst. 'Jim! He's dead! There ain't no point in looking. Birdy's dead. He's gone. Come on!'

With that, I fell back and just lay there. My brother carried on like I weren't there at all, crawling round in the mud on all fours. Then he stopped stock still, turned real slow, then rushed at me. I don't mind saying it scared me some, an I flinched back. Jim didn't notice, or didn't care none.

'Noggin,' he shouts. 'Little Noggin. It's me, Jim.'

He took hold of my shoulders and looked right into my eyes. His face was a mess of mud an blood an that, and I didn't want to look back, but I did. Then I saw them eyes. Jimmy's eyes. They was shining and wide, an I felt my lip starting to shake. Then I pushed my face into his tunic.

'Jim,' I says. 'Jim. Oh, Jim.'

He let go of my shoulders. I pulled my head up to look at him. His eyes flicked left then right, then back at me, an he grinned.

'They can't get me, Noggin. They can't get me,' he says, turning his gaze to something in his hand. 'Not the Hun nor the Devil nor any other begger. Look!'

I looked at what he was holding. It were mostly covered in mud an that, but I could see a patch of brown leather.

'Jim...' I says.

'Look,' he says again, pushing the thing at me. 'Just look, will you. I found it.'

I took it off him, and looked it over some. The football. Punctured and bashed about like it had taken the whole impact of a 5.9 inch shell. Misshaped and beaten. I turned back to Jim, and he grabbed it off me again and rubbed at it with his elbow. All the time saying they couldn't get him, look, look.

Squatting down, he groped in his pocket and pulled out Birdy's baccy tin, and the letter he wrote before we came up the Line. He scrunched the letter up in his fist and pushed it at me.

'No point me writing to him,' he says, gritting his teeth. 'He won't care about anything. Except what I tell him about his *real* son. His favourite son!'

His huge hand pushed against my chest. I took the letter, and stumbled back a bit, trying to find some words. But there weren't none. He didn't want none anyhow. He starts his noise again, jumping to his feet and running off, shouting for all to hear.

30. JIM'S FIVE CHANCES

I clambered to my feet and set off after Jim, stooping an praying we weren't going to get hit. As he reached our trench, he stood there looking down and shouting at them below. I could hear Scottish accents shouting back at him to get down. I knowed it were only a matter of time before a Hun bullet found him. And I knowed there weren't no one else going to help. No Birdy. All he had was me, and my useless leg.

Without thinking any more on it, I pulled myself right up and ran. Like I'd never run before in my life, towards my brother. A mortar shell exploded nearby, and its blast pushed me sideways some, twisting my body. I feel the heat starting up my leg. But I weren't going to stop. My leg weren't going to stop me. Not now. Screaming and shouting, I slammed into my brother. I knowed my weight didn't compare to his, and that he were much stronger than me, but right there an then, none of that mattered. As my elbow went into the small of his back, I heared him gasp, and feeled him buckle in front of me. The ground fell away from under us, an we tumbled down into the trench.

'Jim,' I shouts, getting on my knees in the mud an grabbing his lapels.

He stares me right in the eye, lying there half covered in the muddy water at the bottom of the trench. He's got that look in his face, like he's going to lose it, an his voice goes all quiet and deep.

'You don't get it, do you?' He says, bashing his chest with the football. 'It's all my fault. Your leg and everything. I was supposed to be looking after you that day. Me.'

'Don't Jim,' I says, shaking my head an shutting my eyes. 'Don't.'

'You're the brainy one,' he carries on. 'When I'm with him, all he does is talk about you. You're the one who was going to be the great engineer, not me.'

Then his voice cracked, an went real quiet.

'Dad ain't never going to forgive me for letting you fall that day. Not ever.'

Still clutching the football an Birdy's baccy tin, he twisted and curled up, so I were left looking at the top of his head. I gulped for a breath as his body started to shake, slowly at first, then more. I put a hand out and rested it on him, like he'd done to me often enough. Then them huge shoulders rised up an fell down again, over an over, as he sobbed, louder and louder.

'It's alright, Jimmy,' I tries to say. 'It's okay now. We's alright. We's alright.'

His head snapped up, flicking mud at me. I pulled back, took by surprise. His whole face was white an shaking, and his eyes was wide, wide open. Too wide. He were looking in my direction, but that stare didn't hold no knowing of me. None at all.

'It's alright,' he repeats back at me, getting to his feet. 'It's alright, everyone. I found it!'

Some of them Kilties turned to look, quick, swinging their guns round.

'Okay mate,' says one of them. 'No need to get excited.'

But Jim didn't pay no heed. His shouting got worse, going on about how he found the ball. And about no-one being able to get him, an saying they could try but it were a waste of their time. They couldn't get him. I tried to calm him, putting my hands out an begging him to just sit down again. But it were like I weren't even there to him. And I knowed he were too strong for me to stop him myself.

Jim's shouting turned into just a load of noise. He ran off down the trench, booting the tat of leather along the mud. I started after him, but he just swinged round and ran back the other way, straight past me.

'Jimmy,' I shouted. 'Jimmy, don't. Please.'

An officer appeared. Comed along on account of all the commotion to see what was going on.

He were young. Older an me, of course, but too young for an officer, I reckoned. His face were pasty white under a peaked cap that was too big for his head.

'What's going on here?' He asked. 'What's the matter with that soldier?'

I rushed up to him before anybody could tell him anything. He flinched, pulling his dainty hands up as I got close, and I remembered he was an officer. I tried to do a salute, but it weren't my best effort.

'He's okay, sir,' I told him. 'Just a bit over excited is all. Had a hard time out there. He's fine though. I'll take care of him.'

'Well,' he says, watching Jim running about. 'You're not doing a very good job so far, soldier. Stop him from that, or I'll have him on a charge before he knows it. Quickly now.'

But I were too late. Jim came rushing up, and shouted right in the officer's face.

The officer ordered Jim to stop, and I tried to pull my brother away. But it didn't work. The officer's face got more and more flushed, as he backed away. In the end, he turned round and shouted at the Jocks.

'This man is on a charge,' he said. 'Seize him immediately.'

'Seize him immediately,' Jim copied, then laughed.

Some of the Scots gathered round, but they didn't grab Jim straight away, even though they'd been told to. The officer backed off some more, pushing himself behind them. I could see him unbutton his pistol holster. I don't think Jim noticed. I don't think Jim even knowed he were an officer, or were even there at all.

Soon enough he stopped laughing anyway, and looked to the men around him, slowly like, taking in each face until he comes to mine.

Then it were like something broke inside his body. He dropped to his knees, his body slumping back onto his heels. All the while he was looking at me and his hands was clutching that football and Birdy's baccy tin, tight to his chest. As I looked back at him, his face seemed to change shape. His mouth turned down at the edges, lips shaking. All caked in mud and blood. And he broke down an cried.

The Jocks all looked to each other, then at me. I walked slowly forward and kneeled down with my big brother and put my arms around them broad shoulders. His whole body was shaking, every muscle tight as a drum. I just held onto him.

Soon, the redcaps arrived. Military Police. Three of 'em, thinking to arrest Jim and trying to get hold of him. But that just caused Jim to start shouting again.

'You ain't getting me,' he says, though his voice was high and broken with gasps for breath. 'None of you is getting me.'

He flayed about, waving his ball and tin at everyone. Nothing I said nor done made no difference. In the end, he had to be wrestled down and shackled. The redcaps, and three or four Jocks an all. All through it, I were trying to calm him.

'It's okay Jimmy,' I says to him, over and over. 'It's alright.'

But it weren't, were it? Jim reckoned he had five chances. And he were right. He survived the Hun, same as me. But as to the rest. Well, it seemed to me Jim was killed, wounded, prisoner, all the lot. The flamin' lot, all rolled in one.

Jim was mad.

They held him down in the mud and he just lay there, shaking and sobbing and repeating things over and over.

'I want to go with him,' I said. 'Can't I go with him. See he's alright?'

'You don't want to be thinking like that, sonny,'

one of the redcaps says as they herded Jim off. 'Deserting your post's a firing squad offence. Ain't you seen what's coming?'

I stared. My brother's huge body disappeared round the trench corner.

When I turned back, one of the Kilties stabbed a thumb towards the parapet, and I seed a load of the Jocks was all up on the firing step again, their Smellies pointing over. What really caught my eye, mind, was that they had their heads up, looking over the top. That didn't make no sense. They was going to get shot by Fritz snipers acting like that. I asked what were happening, but they paid no heed, just carried on gawping. Slowly, I lifted myself up, on tiptoes. I knowed it was crazy, but I wanted to see what they was all looking at.

It took a moment for my brain to work it out. I were expecting it to look like it did when we first went over the top. Clouds of smoke, and them coal hills an that. But it was different now. Right across my view, at the base of them spoil heaps, there were a grey line. A dull, tight cloud, slowly moving towards us over the field. Then I twigged what I were looking at, and my heart thumped. Counter-attack. The Hun was coming back at us. Row after row of 'em. Thousands an thousands.

I slumped back down, and leaned against the

trench wall, as their artillery barrage boomed out.

Looking down, I seed I still had Jim's letter in my hand. I knowed there weren't much time, men running about with whistles and bells an shouting starting up all over. I didn't care. They could all wait. The Hun, the Officers, the Sergeant Majors, the Jocks. The barrage. Bombs an bullets. Just wait.

Real slow, I uncurled the scrunched up paper, and stared at it. On the envelope it were addressed to *Mam and Dad,* and our home address in the railway works village. A million miles away. The envelope weren't stuck down or nothing, so I pulled out the sheet of paper and looked at it. It were blank. Both sides. Not a word.

My shoulders sagged. I let out a long breath of air an shoved the letter into my pocket, where mine were.

After clasping my hands together to make sure Emma's gloves was on proper, I checked the magazine and bayonet on my Smelly, an went to rub my leg. As it happened it weren't feeling too stiff.

It were a good leg day.

Behind the story

Noggin's tale is a fictional account of many boy's stories from World War One (also known as the First World War, or the Great War). The story was inspired by a poem called 'The Chances', by Wilfred Owen. Owen was an officer in the Manchester Regiment and was tragically killed on 4th November 1918, exactly one week before the fighting stopped.

In the first verse of Owen's poem, five soldiers are in a trench talking about what they think their chances will be in a battle due to start the following morning. The second verse reveals that one of them is killed, one is wounded, one is taken prisoner, one survives and one goes mad. In his poem, Owen tried to capture the language of the 'Tommy' (a nickname for an ordinary soldier). This book has used the same idea. However, the soldiers Owen fought alongside were from the Manchester area, whereas this book has portrayed lads from Swindon, who join and serve in their local regiment, the Wiltshire Regiment.

The fighting which Noggin and his friends are in is very loosely based on the battle of Loos (a town in France), which Swindon men of the Wiltshire Regiment did take part in. The battle took place in September 1915, and it is estimated that the British suffered some 60,000 casualties in just three days.

The Chances

Wilfred Owen (1893 - 1918)

I 'mind as how the night before that show
Us five got talking'; we was in the know.
'Ah well,' says Jimmy, and he's seen some scrappin',
'There ain't no more than five things as can happen, -
You get knocked out; else wounded, bad or cushy;
Scuppered; or nowt except you're feeling mushy.'

One of us got the knock-out, blown to chops;
One lad was hurt, like, losin' both his props;
And one – to use the word of hypocrites –
Had the misfortune to be took by Fritz.
Now me, I wasn't scratched, praise God Almighty,
Though next time please I'll thank Him for a blighty.
But poor old Jim, he's livin' and he's not;
He reckoned he'd five chances, and he had;
He's wounded, killed, and pris'ner, all the lot,
The flamin' lot all rolled in one. Jim's mad.

From: *The War Poems of Wilfred Owen*, edited by Jon Stallworthy, published by Chatto & Windus, 1994. With thanks to the Wilfred Owen Association.

About the author

Mike Pringle often spent school holidays with the Royal Artillery on Salisbury Plain. His father, who was a gunnery instructor, arranged for him to have a taste of military life, even letting him fire 'twenty-five pounder' artillery guns. However, although Mike enjoyed the excitement of the army, his desire to take a more creative route led him into design, history and writing.

In a career which has included various aspects of arts and heritage, Mike has produced material for He-Man, Transformers, Puddle Lane and Thomas the Tank Engine. And, as well as many years in the museum world, Mike has designed and/or illustrated non-fiction books for Collins, the BBC and Usborne (including a series which won Young Science Book of the Year).

For several years Mike found himself at the Royal Military College of Science. There he helped the military with Virtual Reality and developed computer graphics systems for exploring the past, for which he was made a Doctor in Computing Information Systems Engineering.

Outside work, Mike has enjoyed parascending, abseiling, shooting, running and motor-cycling. He also has a black belt in karate and co-authored and illustrated the Junior Guide to Karate. He now lives in Swindon with his wife, Claire, and Peb the dog.

Also by Mike Pringle:

Paperback: 160 pages **Publisher:** The History Press
ISBN-10: 0750956100 **ISBN-13:** 978-0750956109

More about the Great War

BBC

http://www.bbc.co.uk/schools/0/ww1/
http://www.bbc.co.uk/history/0/ww1/

British Library

http://www.bl.uk/world-war-one
http://www.bl.uk/world-war-one/articles/childrens-experiences-of-world-war-one

Imperial War Museum

http://www.iwm.org.uk/exhibitions/iwm-london/first-world-war-galleries

National Archives

http://www.nationalarchives.gov.uk/first-world-war/

Wikipedia

http://en.wikipedia.org/wiki/World_War_I

And Wilfred Owen

http://www.wilfredowen.org.uk